I0788537

VADIM: CORRUPT

A CLUB XXX NOVEL: BOOK FIVE

LANA SKY

ACKNOWLEDGMENTS

Thanks so much to everyone who supported this draft along the way, including the many beta readers who provided encouragement along the way! Please keep in mind that this story includes dark, graphic, and explicit content matter that is not suitable for readers under the age of 18—or for readers who are uncomfortable with the following subject matter: explicit sex, mentions of sexual abuse, mentions of child abuse, graphic depictions of violence, and mentions of self-harm.

CHAPTER ONE

There is a reason why, when most people climb from their rock bottom, they tend to promise themselves some variation of—*never again.* Never will they reach that low point again, and especially not at the whims of someone else.

Only a fool like me would promptly forget those internal vows the second they fall for a pretty face with a nice wallet. *And* incredible sex. That's the hurtful part—in exchange for a few welcomed distractions, Vadim Gorgoshev made me disregard my list.

My creed.

And I fully deserve the reality bitch-slap coming my way. Ironically, said slap is delivered in the form of a child so beautiful it almost hurts to look at her head-on. With every passing second, I'm reminded of the man standing nearby who manipulated me into this position.

And deep down, I know that I can't even truly be angry with him.

Not when I'm the idiot who failed myself.

"I'm so glad that you and Magdalene can finally meet in person," a dark-haired woman standing in the doorway says warmly. I vaguely remember her name as being Ms. Anderson—the subject of one of Vadim's so-called "business meetings." Now, her real identity is painfully clear as she places her hand on the girl's shoulder and urges her forward with a gentle nudge—*social worker.* "Say hello, Magda," she prompts.

Magda. A creature so small, her limbs are more delicately shaped than even Vadim's. Pale skin enhances her frailty—gosh, she really could be a living doll. A doll dressed in hand-me-downs. I recognize the ill-fitting shape of her simple black shirt and gray skirt—an anomaly I file away for later. Looking at her, it's hard to focus on anything else but the unease setting my face on fire.

A thin headband restrains a mass of wayward curls, but stubborn strands have slipped through anyway to frame her cherub cheeks. Curls every bit as stubborn as her frown. It's like looking at a mini-Vadim, scowling at the world, mistrustful and calculating. Even of her father, it seems. Her eyes flicker over him, devoid of recognition, and confusion mingles with the anger building beneath my skin.

"Magda…" Vadim's voice is a rasp that tugs at something inside me, even as fury simmers hot. He takes a step forward and extends his hand only to let it fall when she crosses her arms—deliberately, I suspect. "Welcome," he grates, letting his hands dangle uselessly at his sides. His eyes dart around the room as if hunting for anything he could direct the conversation to. Lost, he stammers. "Welcome home. I mean, welcome to—"

"It's okay," Ms. Anderson says gently, displaying the patience that I assume comes with her profession. "We hope this will be a great home for her, too. Care to show us around?"

"Of course." Vadim lurches into motion, guiding them through the lower level. Like a sleepwalker, I find myself straggling behind them, watching. Lurking.

It's selfish—I know it is—but my brain plays a horrible game. It takes the features of that beautiful little girl and taunts me with who her mother might be. What she looks like. Someone so alluring that a man as tormented as Vadim took an interest in her. He was careless with her. He trusted *her* with his child.

A child whom, as of five minutes ago, I didn't even know existed.

I stare as they move in a stiff, awkward progression through this clinical, sterile mansion. Magda's appearance alone creates a stark contrast that makes her absence from Vadim's life painfully apparent. Nothing from the color scheme to the sleek architecture lends itself to the idea of a child visiting, let alone living here. But does she? I recall one word Ms. Anderson stated, and my perception is turned upside down for a second time —*placement.* As in adoption?

No one offers up any other explanation. As the small procession makes its way into the kitchen, Ms. Anderson abruptly turns back to the foyer. "I think I'll step out for a minute," she says with a small smile. "I'll grab some paperwork from the car, and you three can use this time to get acquainted."

She leaves, and "us three" take up various positions across the kitchen like opposing generals in a silent war. Vadim hovers near the dining table, his expression stricken. He can't seem to take his eyes off her, Magda. She stands by the bar counter, her arms crossed, her eyes suspiciously narrow.

Gosh, seeing the two of them nearly side by side…

It's breathtaking how identical they look—both in manner and appearance. Simultaneously they embody the two halves of Vadim's personality I've become the most acquainted with. The vulnerable, raw part of him that calls to the empathic part of my soul. And the calculating, vengeful mastermind always one step ahead. With every second ticking by, that selfish, pathetic hurt in my chest digs deeper, biting into my very core.

"Hello, Magda," Vadim manages to say, once again attempting conversation.

She purses her pink lips in a deliberate show of silence, flicking her gaze throughout the room.

"Are you okay?" Vadim adds, and I do a double take. I've never seen him so…off-balance. So out of his element. Helpless, he rakes a hand through his hair, his eyes lacking their calculating cool.

Though Magda seems to possess more than enough for both of them.

"Am I going to live here now?" Her voice is soft, as cold as his can be but lacks any accent. "When I leave the Robinsons?"

"Y-Yes." Vadim fumbles for a chair and sits on it, facing her. "If that is what you want—"

"So, you are a foster family?" Her eyes shift in my direction, inspecting me from head to toe. In some ways, it's the most thorough dressing-down I think I've been subjected to. With a sigh, she turns her attention back to Vadim and cocks her head. "You don't *look* like a foster family."

"Or more," Vadim says thickly. "If that is what you—"

"I hope everyone is getting acquainted," Ms. Anderson declares as she enters the room, a briefcase in tow. "We can go over some of the paperwork, and then Magda, you can visit for as long as you'd like."

"Can I wait in the car?" Magda asks.

"Already?" Ms. Anderson's bright smile strains at the edges. "Don't you want to get to know Mr. Vadim and Ms. Tiffany?"

Magda's blue eyes flash with a hint of emotion that vanishes before I can identify it. "No." She neatly clasps her tiny hands and marches into the hall. A second later, the front door slams shut, and Ms. Anderson collapses onto the nearest chair with a heavy sigh.

"I'm sorry. Magdalene is a wonderful little girl—so brilliant. I mean, you don't know the half. But I won't deny that she has proven to be…challenging lately, especially for her current foster family. Two years ago, and things were wonderful, but it's as if since her illness… Well, she decided to go from a sweet, respectful child into—" She seems to remember her current surroundings and breaks off. Clearing her throat, she shuffles through her briefcase and extracts a handful of documents. "Her placement with her current family ends on Monday," she explains. "They've decided to move back to Michigan after the end of the term, though they did request a meeting with you at your earliest convenience. If it's not too soon, Magda will be ready for placement with you as soon as Tuesday. It is unusual to move so quickly in the process. Still, after the whole teddy bear incident—" she breaks off again and coughs to disguise the action. "Anyway, with the term ending, and Magda's unique health concerns, it could be a challenge to find a suitable family. Thankfully, I see here that you have passed all of the relevant courses."

"Health concerns?" I hear myself croak.

"Yes." Ms. Anderson nods. "She suffers from insulin-dependent diabetes, so she requires a strict dietary regimen and a provider qualified enough to assist with monitoring her sugars regularly. And I'm sure you're aware of the unfortunate setback last year, so her health is a significant factor in finding the right placement. She is also unusually gifted, as you might have been able to tell. Her intellect can make her interactions with some adults… unnerving. For that reason, she requires a very stimulating education that, coincidentally, one of the schools here in Fair Haven, is able to provide. She even received an anonymous scholarship to cover the costs for the duration of her entire schooling, so you can see why keeping her here would be a priority."

Vadim says nothing, his gaze distant. Perhaps he's ruminating over those few key words. *Intelligent. Challenging. Unnerving.* Or, like me, he's marveling at the fact that the description of that child could have easily fit *him.*

"Excuse me," I blurt, unable to hold back any longer. "Where is her mother? Her birth mother?"

"Her m-mother?" Ms. Anderson blinks and glances at Vadim. "Magdalene was discovered abandoned at the age of five, left right on the steps of an orphanage." She shakes her head sadly. "We, unfortunately, have no real information on her birth parents. Adoption would be the aim of this placement, as we have already discussed with Mr. Gorgoshev."

"Of course," Vadim grates, his gaze averted from me. The wall is back up, and I seethe at that, perhaps irrationally. Maybe it's selfish to want something more from him now—some shred of emotion to cling to. Regret? Smugness? *Something.*

"Excuse me." I turn to the door, moving quickly. "I... I have a horrible headache."

Only now does a familiar voice call out, "Tiffany..."

I falter despite myself. He has the nerve to sound hoarse. Tortured. I hear his chair move, but I shake my head. "Don't," I say firmly as I start for the stairs. "Do not follow me."

I make my escape into the bedroom, and I don't stop until I'm barreling into the closet, snatching items from hangers at random. The fact that I own nothing here really doesn't matter in the grand scheme. I selfishly take handfuls of clothing—both his and mine—and shove whatever I can into one of his briefcases. When the case is stuffed to the brim, I take it and march down the stairs. As I descend the final steps, I catch him ushering Ms. Anderson from the door. The second she's gone, he closes it, his back to me.

"Tiffany..."

"What?" I throw the briefcase at him, and it lands harmlessly at his feet. He doesn't even flinch. "Get out of my way."

"What do you want me to say?" he demands, and I stiffen at his tone. The harsh, bitter cadence is a damn near match for Magda's. Their anger is as chilling as their hostility, erected like an invisible brick wall against anyone who dares approach them.

Even if that person has their heart laid bare.

"What should you say?" I hiss incredulously. "Maybe that you have a daughter!"

He's silent, his hand on the doorknob. Despite my anger, a tiny bit of unease bites through, making me falter in my descent. Would he really try to keep me here? Trap me here?

To rebel against that very possibility, I force myself down onto the next step. Then another.

"You have a daughter, and you *abandoned* her," I add to twist the knife, parroting the word Ms. Anderson had used. "You put her in foster care? So now what? You yank her back out? Is that what you wanted your fake wife for? A decoy to game the system to regain custody of your own child? Answer me! I swear to God—"

"She doesn't know I exist."

My shoulders deflate at the raw pain in his tone, and dizzying confusion displaces some of the anger. "So why…"

"I didn't know she did either until two years ago," he explains, turning to face me. His eyes trace the floor rather than meet mine directly. He cradles his temples in the palm of his hands, his jaw clenched. "One day, someone went through great lengths to slip me an envelope that contained only the picture of a five-year-old little girl and her location in an orphanage upstate. I only had to see her face, and I knew. Those eyes…" He shakes his head, clearing away the memory. "There was nothing else— no information on who left her or why. I arranged to have our DNA matched, but the results were no surprise. Afterward, I intervened to have her brought here, where she could receive an education. I secured her safety…"

The raw pain in his voice makes me sway, and I grasp for the banister, gripping it so tightly my knuckles whiten. At the same time, I grit my teeth to keep my expression from faltering. "You learned of her years ago, but you let her go into the foster care system?"

He flinches, leaning against the door as if it's the only thing keeping him upright. "I didn't know what to do. I… I couldn't take care of her—not then." He sounds so earnest about that.

His tone, paired with Ena's vague hints of his mental state, makes me wonder just how unstable he had to be at that point.

It doesn't take rocket science to come up with the answer—so unhinged, he didn't trust himself around his own child.

"And her mother?" I descend another step but don't approach him.

He meets my gaze, and I know whatever he's about to say is anything but a lie. "I can't explain that right now. You need to trust me on that."

But I can't. There's something in how his eyes shift, darkening in that way he does when his wall is up. When he's hiding something. When he's pushing me away.

"A one-night stand?" I prod. Somehow that possibility stings more than him having a genuine relationship. I couldn't convince him to let me suck him off during our first meeting, and yet some other woman managed to snag his child in one go.

Lucky her.

"No," he says, confusing me further. "It is…complicated. More than you can imagine." His jaw clenches in that telltale hallmark of when he's reflecting on that which haunts him the most—his past. As angry as I am now, I can't seem to broach that topic.

So, I do the next best thing and march over to my makeshift suitcase. As I stoop for the strap, his voice rings out.

"Don't."

"Why not?" I hiss, placing my hand on my hip instead. "Give me one reason why I should stay? I didn't sign up for this. You may enjoy treating people like toys, but I won't serve as your smiling Barbie so you can acquire some poor little girl—"

"I can't do this alone. I *can't*." His voice is so guttural each word resonates in my bones, sinking deep. "I can't do this by myself, and I've worked too damn hard to secure her placement. I... I need your help. It's why I wanted to hire..." He grits his teeth, his expression grim with determination. "Stay. I'll give you whatever you want—"

"I want honesty!" I snap, but my voice rings out hollower than I'm used to. Broken. "I want you to tell me more than the basic, generic damn answers. Tell me the truth!"

"I will," he counters, raising his tone to match mine. "I will. But you yourself stated that you had a perfect childhood. I was not so lucky. So do not doubt that my sole concern is Magdalene, and I will do whatever it takes to ensure that she is safe with me."

"Is that a threat?" I try to sound nonchalant—like I'm not afraid. But when he looks as he does now...I am. His eyes blaze, ruthlessly determined.

And not for the first time, I'm forced to reconcile the fact that I have no idea what he's capable of.

"Stay with me," he commands, his voice slightly softer. "I cannot risk losing her to some bureaucratic miscalculation. I've worked too damn hard… The sacrifices I've made for her? You think I've betrayed you, fine. But understand that I can't risk losing her placement. I *can't*."

And he's begging me to prevent just that from happening.

"Fine." Overwhelmed, I lift my hands in surrender. "I'll stay until she's placed with you—but I'm leaving after that."

He sighs in relief. "Thank you—"

"But that is all you're getting out of me," I say over him, desperate to put distance between us—any petty way I can. "Forget our 'relationship.' There isn't one. And I suggest you find somewhere else to sleep. Don't touch me. Don't talk to me. I don't want anything to do with you."

"*S'il te plaît*! Just listen to me…" A groan escapes him, so pained, it stops me right in my tracks. "Tell me what I can do to earn your forgiveness."

"Nothing!" I snarl. Why am I so angry? I still don't know. Or maybe I just can't admit it, even to myself—a stinging pinch in my chest reveals the answer anyway. Jealousy. Jealousy. *Jealousy.*

It festers on a million different petty observations. Like how he listened to me pine for a child I'll never have, while hiding his own. A child connected to him in ways I suspect he's deliberately not revealing—her mother's identity, for one. *Those eyes,* he said in that hollow tone reserved only for those who matter most to him, like his horse Zzazza. *I only had to see her face, and I knew. Those eyes…*

The mere thought of him withholding something from me hurts in ways I can't explain. Tears spill from my eyes as I whirl to face him, my voice scathing, "I escaped a marriage with one self-centered asshole. I'll be damned if I'm jumping into another with someone ten times worse, fake or not. Jim didn't pretend to be anything other than a prick. So, fuck off, Vadim. I suggest you continue your search for a fake fiancée."

I turn on my heel and leave him there. Storming into the bedroom, I slam the door behind me so fiercely the sound echoes like a gunshot.

Then I sink onto the bed and cry in earnest, like I haven't in a very, very long time. Shoulders shaking, voice breaking, full-throttle sobs. It's a pity party, for sure. I can admit that. But it's surprisingly painful to go from wanting someone so much—despite every last warning sign—to knowing that it's better to have nothing to do with him.

And yet still craving him all the same.

Hope can be such a bitch.

CHAPTER TWO

I 'll never forgive myself for who I became during my marriage
—a doormat. Not only did Jim completely obliterate my
self-esteem, but he convinced me during the process that it was
entirely my fault. For so long, I believed that lie…

And one of my promises to myself after the divorce was that no
one would hurt me and walk away scot-free ever again. Thus, my
list was born—the series of goals I've managed to uphold despite
a lifetime of failed ambition and broken dreams.

And the most important one? No relationships.

Being spurned by someone like Vadim is exactly what I deserve
for forgetting that key vow. For ever forgetting that *my* needs
come first now. Always. While the good lord encouraged
forgiveness, the Bible did mention that little thing about an eye
for an eye.

Therefore, I intend to gouge out Vadim Gorgoshev's entirely
guilt-free. Step one? I wake up alone and enter the closet with
only one goal in mind—finding the most revealing, skin-tight,

sluttiest ensemble I can without risking the integrity of my piercing. Screw it. I wear a lacey, see-through bustier and short black tweed skirt that rides up my hips, avoiding pressure on my healing flesh.

Later I'll reflect on the utter stupidity of letting a virtual stranger pierce my nether regions in the first place. At the moment, revenge is a far more appealing animal. To enhance my look, I leave my hair down and skip a bra entirely.

Mr. Billionaire eat your heart out.

No one will ever again make me feel worthless, as if my only value is at their disposal.

I am a queen. So, I do my makeup in the style of one, and when I finally leave the room, I'm ready for war. Irritatingly, I don't find my opponent when I venture downstairs. In the kitchen, all I discover is a lone croissant resting on a plate beside a bowl of fresh fruit. As subtle a peace offering that a smug bastard could present without eating crow.

Whatever. I ignore it in favor of scouring the rest of the house in search of him.

I toy with the prospect that he didn't sleep here at all, ceding this battlefield to me—but then I spot him in the study, slumped over his desk. And a teensy, tiny bit of doubt creeps in, poisoning my heart with...concern. Gone is the calculating, smug businessman. This creature, with his eyes closed and features gaunt, is the epitome of exhaustion.

My fingers twitch rebelliously. Anger takes a backseat for a split second, surrendering to the emotion only he can inspire in me. I have a sudden urge to smooth the hair back from his face and encourage him to go to bed.

I take a step forward… And a tendril of light from the window enhances the planes of his face—and how identical they are to his daughter's. My anger renewed, I loudly storm back into the kitchen and slam my way through cupboards and drawers until he appears in the doorway, his eyes bloodshot. His gaze settles on my face first, his lips parting. "We need to talk—"

"Or not." I down a glass of orange juice as I snatch up the croissant and head for the stairs.

He doesn't follow me, and I spend the rest of the day avoiding him, too terrified that the sight of him may make me break.

And after seven years of cowering, I *refuse* to break.

Sleep provides only a brief reprieve. As soon as dawn creeps over the horizon, I steal a pair of masculine sweats from the closet and a set of tennis shoes for good measure. Desperate for fresh air, I head downstairs, but I barely make it through the front door before I sense him behind me.

"Where are you going?"

Gosh, he sounds more haggard than yesterday. I turn to face him and once again feel my resolve being tested. His dress shirt is rumpled, suspiciously resembling the one he wore two days ago. His pants are a wrinkled mess, and his hair sticks out at odd angles—no doubt assaulted all night by raking fingers. He looks so tired. So worn.

With difficulty, I flick my gaze from him and escape into the chilly, dawn morning.

"I'm going for a walk," I tell him coldly. A part of me flinches at my tone. *Chill out, Tiffy.* Again, I can't understand why I'm so angry. Why a sick part of me thrills at making him flinch. Survival instinct? Maybe. I'll guard my heart at all costs from him, even if it kills me. "Don't follow me," I add as I slam the door.

Driven by nervous energy, I explore his property with a singular focus and find myself surprised by how big it is. And at the same time, just how empty it seems. He must control acres and acres, their boundary defined by wooden posts placed at seemingly random intervals. The house itself overlooks a wide pool set in gray stone as well as a private dock and a vacant boathouse. There's even an empty, lonely stable at the back overlooking a view of the waterfront.

It's a home that any little girl would dream of living in, and yet it's almost entirely devoid of anything she might want to do. There is no playground. No dollhouse. No sea of toys to drown herself in.

It's as if the man found the perfect blueprint for a family home but had absolutely no clue how to fill it. And now the clinical emptiness of the house makes more sense—he's stuck, torn between who he is at his core, and the man he seemingly *wants* to be.

A father.

If I weren't so angry with him, I'd gently suggest he work some color into the décor. Build a swing set and maybe a garden for her to play in. Does he even have a room picked out for her?

Yes, I suspect, recalling the one upstairs that he requested I avoid. But something tells me that even it is empty. Was he expecting his fake wife to lend him expertise in that arena? It sounds so stupid—a man like him with so many resources could easily hire someone to help him design a little girl's room. At the same time, it fits. Vadim is so cripplingly self-conscious, he wouldn't trust anyone to help. Not even me, the woman who bared her soul to him. Who claimed to want a relationship with him.

Who now hates him.

I reinforce that last statement as I return to the house dripping sweat, only to find an unfamiliar vehicle in the driveway—a stocky, serviceable minivan. When I ease open the front door, a sharp voice reaches my ears, and I hesitate over the threshold, straining to listen.

"…so, you can see why we were concerned," a woman says, her tone shrill and haughty. "We love and nurture children of all ages, shapes, and sizes, but I hope you are prepared for that girl."

"She can be…unusual," a man interjects, his voice slightly more tolerable, almost apologetic. "That's what you meant to say, right, honey?"

Rather than sulk upstairs like I should, I follow the conversation into the kitchen, drawn by the tone. It's far too serious than I figure a typical visit would be—not that Vadim seems like the afternoon brunch type anyway.

I find him seated at the table, impeccably dressed in an ebony suit. Across from him are two strangers—the minivan owners, I assume. The woman wears a hideous sweater ensemble, her blond hair pulled back severely into a bun, while the man wears a faded suit and sports a thinning brown mustache. They certainly don't look like the type to consort with a billionaire in his private estate.

Unless…

They're Magda's current foster placement.

As I falter near the doorway, the woman looks at me, her gaze honed sharp. "Oh, is this your wife?"

"Tiffany," Vadim says by way of explanation, though he isn't looking in my direction. His gaze is solely focused on a pile of documents scattered before him—the supposed topic of this meeting. "These are the Robinsons," he adds, his tone crisp. "Magdalene's current foster family."

Ah. I struggle to resume my fake wife ruse and force a grin, tucking my wild hair behind my ears. In a heartbeat, I channel my mother, my anger pushed aside—for now. "Pleased to meet you," I say charmingly. "I apologize for my appearance. I must have lost track of time."

"Oh, it's no worry. And I don't want to be rude…" Mrs. Robinson wrings her hands together, her lips pursed. The judgmental part of me recognizes the expression for what it is—a pent-up busy body about to unload. "It's just, I have to ask, did Angela tell you *everything*? I know Magdalene is only a child, but I insisted upon a higher level of care for her. Perhaps… psychiatric in nature. I know it's not politically correct to insinuate—"

"I am fully prepared to take her," Vadim says sternly. It's strange. His entire expression is a carefully constructed mask of utter politeness. But something in his gaze makes me shiver. I step forward, claiming the chair beside him.

"Yes," I say, squaring my shoulders in a show of solidarity. "We're ready."

Poor Mrs. Robinson swallows hard and shifts in her seat, laughing nervously. "Yes, well… Honey, tell them." She nudges the man beside her. "Tell them about the *incidents*."

"Magda has only been with us a year, mind you," Mr. Robinson admits with a heavy sigh. "And she had already been through so much, what with her health problems. We knew she'd need some time to adjust—"

"She's terrorized the other children," Mrs. Robinson blurts out, folding her hands over the table. "She's damaged property. There's this teddy bear she came with. Well, recently, we discovered that not only did she rip its head off, she then broke into my embroidery kit and sewed it back together with red thread! It's ghastly. We think it was a threat intended to frighten the other children." Horror laces her tone, her voice shaking. "She's incredibly isolative. She won't let you help her with anything. Not her hair. Not with bathing—"

"She's independent," Mr. Robinson cuts in with another apologetic frown.

His wife scoffs. "She's stubborn. The teachers at her school say she hasn't attempted to make any friends—"

"Some children can be shy in social settings," I interrupt, driven by an instinct I can't name to defend a child I don't even know. Internally I scold myself—despite the irritation prickling in my chest, these people can't be all terrible. Can they?

"*That* girl isn't shy," Mrs. Robinson says with a sniff. "And with the cost of her education, you would think they'd try harder to drill some social skills into her curriculum."

"Is that so?" A muscle in my jaw jerks, and I feel my smile twitching. "Well, children do learn by example."

Mrs. Robinson's brows furrow. "I'm sorry?"

"I…" Thinking fast, I try to smooth out my response. "As a teacher, I learned that it's unfair to subject everyone to the same standards."

Somehow, I maintain my polite tone—but it must crack, because both Robinsons flinch. *Good.* My hands are clenching, I realize, my nails digging into my palms. With difficulty, I flatten them against the table, keeping my grin firmly in place.

"Her grades are exemplary," the husband admits with genuine awe.

"That's the thing. She's intelligent to an uncanny degree," Mrs. Robinson says, her nostrils flaring. "*Too* intelligent. She likes to sing creepy little songs in foreign languages—but she refuses to say what they're about. She carries that terrifying bear everywhere she goes. I assumed it was damaged at first and tossed it into the rubbish bin, and she threw a tantrum so fierce we had to call Angela over just to soothe her. A few weeks ago, Richard noticed that someone had been breaking into his office at night, using his work computer. The other children wouldn't dare. When we looked at the search history, we noticed that whoever used it had been looking up drug companies. One of them manufactures a medication Richard takes for a heart condition. What if she was trying to find out some way to—"

"Thank you for coming." Vadim stands and gestures politely toward the foyer, his posture stiff. "I would hate to keep you, given that you are so busy with your other children. I appreciate you stopping by."

"Yes, thank you," I snap, matching his tone as I rise to my feet. From the corner of my eye, I see his hand twitch as if aching to take mine. At first, I deliberately flatten my palm against my side —but then something makes me relent, grasping his.

Together, we start for the foyer, leaving the couple to follow.

Stunned, they blink in unison and share a quick glance. Then they hurry past us as Vadim opens the door.

"Angela is a wonderful social worker," Mrs. Robinson adds as she lingers over the threshold. "I'm sure if you wanted to look into another child…"

That's it. I feel my mask slipping, my grin flattening. If I didn't understand Vadim's determination to gain custody of Magdalene before, I do now. While unsure, he'll strive to be a better provider to her than these people could ever be.

As if he's reading my mind, a muscle in his jaw twitches, and Mrs. Robinson promptly scuttles after her husband. I join him in watching them leave, my thoughts swirling. On the one hand, they seem like the breed my mother used to loathe back in Cali —overly conservative busybodies. At the same time…

The child they painted seems well beyond the skill set of an ex-Sunday school teacher and an emotionally withdrawn businessman. Does he have any idea what he might have gotten himself into? I glance at him, surprised to discover that…*yes*, he does. His jaw is set, more determined than ever.

And in that lone expression, I see a hint of his daughter, and any doubt dies. Two creatures, easily misunderstood, requiring patience to read. Understand. Love. My fury returns, but wavers the longer I watch him, imagining him with Magdalene, unraveling her own guarded layers. The second he catches me staring, his expression softens, his voice rasping, "Tiffany, wait—"

But I don't. Releasing him, I turn and head straight up to the bedroom, my heart racing.

Damn. Damn. Damn!

CHAPTER THREE

It shouldn't be so hard to maintain my anger toward him. Within the space of a few minutes, my thoughts have turned from *"make him pay"* to... *"listen to him, you stubborn bitch."* Fighting to regain my resolve, I shower and change into a sinfully revealing negligee and a barely visible thong that by some miracle doesn't snag on my healing piercing. Both make for impenetrable armor in this silent war, and when I strut back into the hallway, I'm determined to win the last battle at all costs.

And I nearly run into Vadim. But he's...different. It's as if the pleading man from downstairs transformed into a stranger in an instant. A disinterested stranger. His eyes skim over me with barely any notice as he promptly enters a nearby room.

And I nearly trip as my head whips around, tracking him. *What the hell?*

The room is the same one he pierced me in, I see as I follow him, driven by sadistic curiosity. What could distract him from his groveling?

Redecorating, it seems. The leather chaise is now against one of the walls, the medical instruments vanished. One of those heavy boxes lies open in the center of the room while Vadim rummages through it, apparently assembling something. It's large and black made of wood. A table?

Square-shaped and about waist-high, it contains a divot with a soft cushion covered in red fabric and two silver fixtures on either side. A detail so unusual, I find myself inching forward just to make sure my eyes aren't playing tricks.

Nope. The closer I come, the easier it is to identify those objects, positioned upright, made of silver rings—manacles.

And something inside me is brutally savaged by a wave of jealousy so fierce I sway.

"Preparing for your new fake wife?" I ask nastily, grasping for any form of retaliation.

He doesn't even look at me. Instead, he peers at a white booklet that I assume must be instructions. Then he adjusts something at the end of the odd platform with a silver wrench. He's changed, stripping his suit for the white dress shirt and slacks. The look, paired with his current task, makes something inside me quiver, my throat dampening. *Damn.* He makes a buttoned-up Mr. Handyman look sexy.

But I'm not fooled.

To prove as much, I stomp loudly downstairs and steal one of Ena's meals from the freezer. I eat while scowling and contemplate taking one of his fancy sports cars and attempting once more to send the poor man into bankruptcy.

Instead, I find myself bounding right back upstairs and towing the boundary of that mysterious room. He's still here, assembling yet another unknown wooden structure. Sweat glistens on his brow, and he's left the first few buttons of his shirt undone, exposing the scar along his throat. He looks so intent on his task, he doesn't seem to notice me until I strut boldly to the platform.

Up close, I start to get an inkling of what it might be, and my heart skips a beat. The red cushion is the ideal size and width to comfort a woman's torso if, say she happened to be leaning across it—and those manacles are in the perfect position to capture her wrists and keep her immobile.

Like some sexy, taboo pillory.

My heart sinks, poisoned by yet even more jealousy. I swear, my vision goes green. I can't help myself. Like any scorned creature, I attempt to go right for his jugular.

"Nice to see that your research into kink won't end with me," I say coldly, placing my hand down within his line of sight. I can't stop myself from fingering the curve of one of the manacles as burning hot envy unfurls in my chest. So much for his supposed ignorance when it comes to kink. He seems to be well prepared to welcome his next conquest and indulge her fully. "I hope your new fake wife is a prude—"

He snatches my wrist before I can truly process the action. With an easy display of strength, he flattens my palm against the platform. *Clink.* The manacle encircles my wrist and stunned, I tug, surprised when it doesn't budge.

"What the hell?"

He grabs my other wrist and secures it within the other manacle just as quickly. Then he backs away from the platform entirely, escaping my limited view. Panic sends my heartbeat racing as I crane my neck, desperate to track his movements.

"What the hell are you doing? Vadim!" My voice rings out, trembling with a hint of uncertainty. "Vadim!"

Within seconds, he reappears directly across from me, dragging a black stool behind him. Calmly, he sits, placing his hands on either knee. Our gazes meet, and a tendril of unease races down my spine. I'm suddenly aware of my new piercing, grazing my clit, enhancing the burning sting I've barely grown accustomed to. But it's anything but painful. Stubbornly, I strive to ignore the sensation in favor of baring my teeth at him.

"Get me out of this!"

He cocks his head to the side and leans back on his stool. I sense that he's waiting for something—like a dog trainer waiting for the naughty mutt to remember one command or the other.

"You fucking bastard!" I strain at my binds, hissing in exasperation. "Let. Me. Go!"

Something unreadable flashes through his dark eyes, and I stiffen, falling silent. A subtle softening of his jaw is my reward, and I watch, riveted as he lifts one of his hands and lowers it to his fly.

With envious dexterity, he has it open in seconds, palming his cock. *Holy crap.* He moves slowly in firm, deliberate strokes that have him hardening in a shocking display that leaves me gasping.

"W-What are you doing?" I try to sound angry, but awe laces my tone instead. *Shit. Shit. Shit.* I *want* to seethe, and rage, and scream.

But he is impressive even from this angle. His piercing stands erect, swallowed by the swelling flesh until the rounded ends of the barbell are all that remain visible.

Well aware of my drifting attention, his eyes ruthlessly seek mine out as he manipulates his straining cock. Stroke after stroke leaves him pulsating, but his expression remains unchanged. Unreadable. Cold. Undeniably sexy…

No. "S-Stop!" I shake my head and struggle against my binds, making the metal clang. "What the hell are you doing?"

He *does* stop, his hand stilling, his gaze unmoving. For seconds. Longer. Unbearably long. I squirm, my lips parting for another demand.

The second they do, he starts to stroke himself again, rendering me silent. As my lips close, he strokes faster. Again. Soon, his entire body is rocking with the motion, his cock straining in his grasp. Beautiful doesn't even begin to describe the sight. Any words die in my throat as his hand moves even faster. Surer. The longer he pleasures himself, the more I lose my train of thought.

Men like him don't exhibit themselves lightly. It's an intentional display, I suspect. Meant for me alone. To tease me. Shatter me. Chastise…

And it's cruel, unusual punishment. I'm senseless, lost in the whirlpool of conflicting emotions. Shame. Rage. *Need.* Musings of anger quickly turn to imagining how he would taste, let alone feel if I tried to take him from this angle. As if reading my mind, he stands, letting his pants fall down to his ankles, baring himself completely. Slowly, he advances, his hand still moving, muscles straining beneath his skin.

I don't even realize that my mouth is already open until he cups my chin, tilting it so that I'm forced to look up at him. His thumb traces my lower lip as he bucks his hips. And I don't hesitate.

A groan rips through me as his taste explodes over my tongue, and I eagerly lap at the crown. My eyes roll, and I forget all about hating him. Fellating him on the bed was one thing. But this…

It's so different.

The angle forces him deeper, and I have to tilt my throat to better accept his length. Bound and immobile, all I can do is take whatever he's willing to give. Just the tip at first. Then the full crown. More. More.

More.

I gasp in exasperation as he pulls away, but then our eyes meet. As if in warning, he caresses my cheek before guiding himself in, in, in.

My eyelids flutter as I struggle to handle this much. He's throbbing against my tongue, so thick I can barely close my lips around him.

And it's utter perfection.

I hum in contentment as he rocks his hips, feeding me more, precious bit by precious bit. My wrists strain against the manacles as pressure builds between my legs, seeming to center right over my piercing. I start to whimper as he cradles my cheek while easing more into my mouth, barely teasing the back of my throat.

Then he withdraws again, leaving me gasping.

Before I can even protest, his fingers work to part my hair as he encircles my position. His other hand finds my waist and toys with the waistband of my thong. I shiver. The slightest pressure teases the piercing and sets off a tidal wave of friction, unlike anything I've ever felt. Unprepared, I writhe, torn between clamping my knees against the heat or opening myself up to him further.

"How did I know this method would reach you when words don't?" He sounds so damn smug. I hiss, only to trail off as he teases me again with another gentle swipe. Another and I moan in hapless surrender.

"You wore this to tease…" His voice is a guttural shadow of his usual neutral cadence. Still calm, but nowhere near as disarming. Lust lurks in the vicious tone, heightening the heat building in my blood. "Didn't you?"

I shake my head, gritting my teeth against a reply as I struggle to remember my anger. "Go to hell—"

I gasp as his finger slips between my legs, teasing the moisture gathered there. "It's working," he grates. "Consider this me teased to the point of madness…"

A part of me stiffens, aware of my healing piercing—but the pain doesn't hurt, and I'm reckless enough to writhe, just enough to test my limits. More pressure sets me ablaze.

And it's too tempting to heed common sense warning me to stop.

I wantonly rock my hips, seeking out the contact. In response, he teases me with the tip of one elegant finger, and my brain explodes. I buck against him, seeking out more.

I'm denied. The finger withdraws only to tug my thong down my hips entirely. Cool air tickles the heated flesh, and I shiver as his touch finds my ass, kneading the right cheek.

"So beautiful." He practically groans the praise, his voice thickening. "So wet. Beg me for mercy, and perhaps I'll grant it."

Even as his groping fingers churn my brain into butter, I manage to cock my head back and laugh. "Beg? …Screw…you!"

His hand withdraws only to strike again in a stinging burst of pain—he spanked me. My tongue moistens my lips as my thoughts go on hiatus. His palm is already stroking the pain away, but just as I relax, he smacks me again. *And again.*

"I will redden this flesh," he promises darkly. "That's what you want, isn't it? My beauty, so damn stubborn. I warned you that only you have ever driven me to *this*. Chastisement." Another smack makes me lurch against my binds, a whine trapped in my throat. "Do you require more?"

Yes. "N-No," I attempt to hiss. "Get off—"

Unbearable friction teases my mound—thick, pulsating pressure rubbing against me, carelessly close to my piercing. I go rigid, my thoughts self-destructing. The resulting pleasure is almost too good. Too dangerous. My brain can't handle it. It wipes itself blank, a slave to the whims of his movements. His sadistic game.

Groaning, he parts my lower lips around his shaft, sliding through my wetness only to pull back. Again. Back. Again.

It's maddening.

My lips seem to move of their own accord, spitting out pleas my brain never approves of.

"Please," I whisper, arching into him as much as I can. What I'm begging for? I don't know. Just that I need more of…this. His touch. His appreciative grunts as I eagerly buck into his fingertips. More of him.

"You want me inside you?" he wonders, his tone a rasp.

I can only nod, too far gone for shame. "Yes—"

"You know I can't." He rocks against me anyway, and my eyes roll it feels so good. But he never goes deeper than the slightest, taunting bit of pressure. Out of concern? My piercing is on fire, but in a way that only enhances the pleasure shooting through me in an electric pulse.

"Please—"

"You want relief?" His tone softens even as his grip on my hair tightens sharply, tugging. The act forces my head back, wrenching my gaze to the ceiling. "Do you want to come, beautiful?"

I nod mindlessly, wiggling my hips for more.

"Please…"

His cock disappears, leaving me so aching I cry out. Another pressure eagerly replaces his full length—smaller and more persistent. His thumb? He eases the tip inside me before going deeper.

And my binds are the only things keeping me from levitating. *Piercing. Pleasure.* Those two words dance through the remains of my lust-addled brain. Holy goodness, I never knew that even fingering could feel this good. The slightest penetration enhances the pressure swelling over my clit—one teasing thrust and combustion.

My orgasm rips through me so fiercely I don't even realize it's happening until I hear my own cries echoing back to me. My nails scrape against the wood beneath them, my body trembling with ecstasy.

"I told you once… You are *owned*," I hear Vadim claim, his voice gruffer than ever. Possessive. *I should fear it,* a part of me warns. At the moment, I'm too far gone to care.

"Owned," he continues, still stroking me from the inside out. "Cherished. Chastised." *Smack!* Another blow to my ass makes me lurch onto the tips of my toes, my core rippling, my brain mush. I lose track of the words spilling off my tongue—just that they would make me blush were I in my right mind.

"Please, please, please—"

He strokes through my hair, murmuring praises as his cock returns, pressing insistently at my mound. My clit is on fire, a searing warning—but all concern of healing timeframes leaves my brain.

"Please!"

He bucks his hips, entering me with such a smooth, controlled thrust that only my sheer wetness drags him as deep as he goes. From the outside, my sore flesh isn't touched at all. But from the inside…

I scream as pleasure tears through me in unbearable waves. Almost too much. Tears sting my eyes, and I slump, mindless as he takes me so, so gently.

"Beautiful," he says, his breaths feathering, thrusts strengthening. "So beautiful… *Mine.*"

I'm boneless when he wrenches himself free and hisses through his own torturous release. Fiery heat spills against my lower back, and my eyes flutter as my brain rockets to cloud nine all over again.

When I finally regain my senses, I'm no longer bound. His fingers trace patterns up and down my arms as his grated voice sinks into my ear.

"So good," he praises. "So beautiful when you come for me… So beautiful."

I face him on jellied legs. Our lips meet. Teeth gnashing, tongues grappling for leverage. I'm in his arms before I know it, grinding against him without a damn for my healing piercing.

"N-No!" Seemingly with difficultly, he pulls back and shoves his hand between us, preventing me from further stimulation. Then he snatches my waist, lifting me into his arms completely.

Dazed, I go limp as he carries me into the master bedroom and then the bath, and finally into the shower. He strips us both of our remaining clothing. Then, one-handed, he programs the water and sets me on the bench, blocking me in with his body to keep me seated.

"Let me clean you off, beautiful," he demands, as the water lashes down.

But I rub my legs together shamelessly, imploring him. "I want more." I barely recognize my voice, rasping with lust. Never in my life have I so wantonly craved anything else. *More.* More pain mixed with pleasure. More teasing. Taunting. *Everything.*

I'm drugged on a kink I never knew existed. And deep down beyond the ecstasy, I know I should be terrified that he holds the keys to it all.

"You'll have more than enough when I'm through with you." He chuckles and sinks to his knees before me, brandishing a cloth and a bottle of soap. I shiver as he pries my legs apart and inspects me, frowning. "But not tonight," he adds sternly. "You need rest. Now stay still so that I can clean you."

A pout tugs on my lower lip, but I'm quickly distracted by his touch as he guides the cloth carefully over my aching frame. It's dizzying how seamlessly he can go from spanking me, to bathing my limbs with the utmost care.

Almost as quickly as I can go from hating him, to practically purring in his arms. In my right mind, I'd be more alarmed by that, I think.

As it is, I go languid beneath his ministrations, and watching him is almost enough to make up for the lack of stimulation. When he's done, he tosses the rag aside, shuts off the water, and returns with an armful of towels that he bundles me in.

Minutes later, we land on the bed, and I eagerly snuggle into him, nuzzling against his chest. "I'm sorry for being such a horrible bitch," I confess, my tone surly.

He sighs, wrapping me in his arms, pulling me close. "You weren't completely horrible."

"Hey!" I playfully slap his chest only to copy his sigh as I eye him through my lashes. His serious expression remains unchanged, even as he strokes through my damp hair. I find myself observing him in full, from the pale skin of his chest to the jagged shape of his scar. I reach out, brushing my finger along the edge of it. It's so long, stretching from his ear down to his collar bone.

I can't even begin to imagine what might have caused it. An accident? Something more violent?

Without offering up an explanation, he lets my finger dance along his skin, but from the set of his jaw alone, I know instinctively not to ask him about it. Not yet, at least. Instead, I turn my attention to something a bit more imminent.

"It's a good thing that you're building a playground just for me," I point out softly. Now those mysterious boxes in that room have a newer significance. "But you need to build one for Magda."

He stiffens, inhaling sharply. I'm finding that it's getting slightly easier to read him. I can peg this reaction to one cause in particular.

"You don't want to talk about her," I surmise. "Not yet."

"No..." He shakes his head, his expression tense. "I will. But this... It is painful for me. I just need time."

"At least you're being honest with me." I reinforce the praise by brushing my fingers down his chest. "That's all I'm asking for. You don't need to tell me everything—but I need to know *something*."

"And you will." He captures my hand and brings it to his cheek. "Just know that... I want this," he confesses hoarsely. "More than anything. I want my daughter to be with me. I want to be a father to her. I want..."

"What changed within two years?" I ask gently.

He frowns and seems to shrug in the same instance. "She almost died," he says. "Last year. She became very sick—an infection entered her bloodstream. You've heard of her condition? It makes any prolonged sickness far worse. She became septic and eventually required a machine just to breathe. For ten days, I spent every minute wondering if I'd lose her for good."

"God..." I picture her frail, fragile appearance and shudder at the thought of her on a vent. I know firsthand how it feels to lose a child—even if I've never met my own—but I can't imagine that level of torment. Thankfully. Swallowing hard, I struggle to form words. "That's awful." I squeeze his fingers tightly, unsure of what else to do. Or say. The only obvious course seems to be just listening—and I suspect that's exactly what he needs. To talk.

"It was the first time I'd seen her in person," he admits, staring ahead, his face blank. "I held her. Sang to her. I touched her cheeks… I watched her fight for her life. But the second she grew well enough to breathe on her own, I left her…" He sighs. "And I did not handle the guilt well." A small, tired smile alludes to the tumult of emotions he only ever lets me get a glimpse of. "One could say I went off the deep end afterward. Only Ena could keep me from doing something foolish—" He frowns at the memory, and I don't have the heart to explore that statement further. Sighing once more, he shifts, holding me more firmly against him. "When I finally came to my senses, I was resolved, however. I *knew* that I had made the right choice. I would continue to fund Magda's education and expenses from afar, but I would keep my distance—it would be better for us both. And I did stay away. Even when events beyond my control forced me to return to this city, I stayed away from her."

"Then what made you change your mind?"

"Maxim," he says coldly. "I had spent months talking myself out of claiming my own child, and in the meantime, Maxim had taken six under his wing, none of them his. It was as if, once again, my 'legitimate' brother was flaunting that superiority right in my face."

"So, you decided to officially adopt Magda?"

"I have no legal claim to her as it stands," he says. "To give her the best life possible, I need to go through the proper channels and jump through whatever hoops the government insists I may. My resources can achieve many things, but, in this case, I cannot rely on them. And while I know that she is biologically mine, for obvious reasons, I cannot claim as much without proof and documentation. For both her sake and mine, this is the easiest way."

"Is that why you wanted a fake wife?"

A lazy smile shapes his mouth for a fleeting moment. "I was interviewing mainly childcare workers," he admits. "Entirely for Magda's sake and not my personal enjoyment. It seems I settled on a candidate the complete opposite to what I initially thought."

"I do have childcare experience," I grudgingly point out.

"I lucked out then," Vadim says, still running his fingers through my hair. "If you will stay, that is. I apologize for not being upfront before."

"It's not like you didn't try," I admit as I parse through my memories of the past few days. There were a handful of moments where he definitely tried to confess something important—and I had obliviously shrugged him off. "But if we are to do this, then no more secrets..."

Even if admitting them out loud stings like hell. Facing him, I force a serious note into my voice. "I need you to understand right now that I'm not sure if I'm really ready for a serious relationship with a child involved. No, actually, I know that I'm not—not that you are either. Magda is your main concern now."

I nod along with my own logic. Laying out such boundaries now makes sense. Exposing myself to a man whose emotions run hot and cold is one thing. Opening myself up to a child, in the same way, isn't fair to either of us.

"I understand," he admits, but when I crane my neck back to observe his face, he's frowning, as surly as ever even with his eyes half-closed.

"But we can still have sex," I add, feeling no shame in making that demand. "At least until Magda is placed with you permanently. After that, we're done. That is what is best for everyone."

Mainly myself, and the struggle of reconciling my newfound lust with my own internal promises. My list. My rules. My creed.

He doesn't mention whether he agrees or not with that assessment. He's silent for so long that it isn't until I look back at him that I realize why—the poor man fell asleep.

CHAPTER FOUR

I wake up just as the sky is setting beneath the waterfront below. It's evening already, though I still feel exhausted beneath a level of sex-drunk energy. Yawning, I disentangle myself from Vadim, and I have to pinch myself just to keep from watching him for hours. His two-day exile from bed resulted in poor sleep, apparently. He's unconscious, his chest rising and falling in a slow, easy rhythm that shatters the guarded persona he so regularly presents to the world.

He's mine like this—a dangerous thought I can't seem to shake. Hoarding his beauty to myself, I take my time lightly stroking the panes of his chest, my mind racing ahead to all the dirty ways I could explore him further.

Eventually, his welfare takes precedence as my own stomach growls in hunger. Sighing, I leave the bed and tiptoe into the closet to steal one of his shirts, opting for more coverage than my lingerie in case I find Ena lurking downstairs. Then, I enter the kitchen to find it empty, and I fix up one of the freezer meals, dividing it among two plates. When I return upstairs, I'm juggling a bottle of orange juice for him and wine for me.

I move cautiously, only to trip over the threshold, and I wind up dropping my wine. It lands with a thud that could wake up the devil himself. Crestfallen, I look at the bed, and sure enough, Vadim is stirring, a lazy hum rumbling in his throat.

"Breakfast?" he wonders, sounding so darn husky my toes curl. His eyes are surprisingly mistrustful, suspicious even. Might I have laced his juice with poison, I imagine him thinking. Do I truly forgive him so easily?

I smirk to feed his paranoia, and a lazy grin shapes his mouth in response, his jaw softening.

"Dinner," I correct, inching forward to set our plates on the bed. I lift a fork from his and stab at a piece of steaming meat. Then I shift onto my knees and crawl toward him. "Open."

He does so with his own amused smirk, allowing me to feed him the first bite. I gape as he chews, and I rush to drag his plate closer and offer him something else.

"I love pampering you," I murmur as he opens his mouth for more.

"I will turn you into a domestic yet," he teases, making my heart skip. "First, I'll get you addicted to my cock, and then I'll have you trained to enjoy feeding me. You'll be far too sprung to leave."

He sounds so confident. Too confident, making the boast sound more like a promise than anything else.

"Is that so?" I scoot back and grab my own plate, sampling a few roasted veggies, leaving him to feed himself. "I'll have you know that I don't think I'd make a very good soccer mom."

Something in my tone makes him shrug the blankets from his frame and stand. I stare as he stretches his bare limbs and pads into the bathroom. I follow him and wind up leaning against the doorway as he steps into the shower.

Cocking his head, he meets my gaze, his eyes flashing. "What was that you promised me once?" he wonders. "Something about sucking me off to show your gratitude…"

"Devil!" I grin wickedly and finger the buttons of my borrowed shirt. "Only if you ask me nicely."

His gaze fixates on my mouth, and I shiver as his tongue traces his lower lip. "I would very much enjoy feeling your mouth on me."

I'm naked within seconds, practically running toward him. The shower spray bastes us with gentle pressure as I follow him to the bench and drop to my knees. Our eyes meet and something unspoken shoots between us, as jolting as electricity.

I take him in without hesitation as he sinks his fingers through my hair, groaning in approval. Eager to push his reaction to the fullest, I grip the base of him, gasping as he thickens, straining against my touch.

The pleasure is so intense my eyes threaten to roll, but… A part of me panics with the increasing realization that watching him watch me is ten times more explosive than any impending orgasm. Our eyes meet again. I lick him. He jumps. I suck. His grip tightens, his eyelids fluttering.

So, I do it again.

And again.

His wall is down, his gaze open, and all I see is a man so beautiful it hurts, looking at me as though I'm a goddess. Desirable. Cherished.

And yet still kept at arm's length.

Still, it's beyond anything newly-divorced Tiffy could have imagined just a few days ago.

I close my eyes, overwhelmed, and put all of my focus into pleasuring him, feeding off the throaty groans that broadcast his enjoyment. Deeper. Rasps. Grunts. I worship him, teasing him with as much of my throat as I dare.

And in the end, I relish his release, drinking him down—every last drop.

It's too good. Panting, I rest my face against his knee, seeking out the comfort of his touch. The sensation of his fingers over my heated flesh feels too damn soothing. A salve I've gone my whole life without needing, healing a pain I never realized ached until this moment.

Dangerous thoughts, Tiffy. With difficultly, I pull away.

"I will forever live in regret of denying myself this," he says. I look up to find him leaning back against the wall of the shower stall, his hair mused, his expression shifting amid another earth-shattering revelation. His fingers graze my cheek reverently, smoothing back my damp hair, and I can't resist settling against him again. "I love the way you suck my cock."

I feel myself blush as my tongue chases every remainder of him from my lips. "Careful, Mr. Vadim. That almost sounds like praise."

He laughs, stroking me absently, his expression utterly content. "Take it as you will, Ms. Connors. I look forward to indulging your other fantasies."

"Oh?" I perk up, my brain skipping ahead. "Such as?"

He chuckles deeply and cradles my jaw, urging me to meet his gaze again. "I will show you," he promises. "I will build you your playground as you call it. But in return? You lend me your expertise."

I raise an eyebrow and rise up to straddle him, inching as close to him as I can. His arms encircle me, forming a cocoon of warmth against the shower spray. "My expertise in what?"

"Children," he says simply. His mouth settles in the crook of my shoulder, nipping. Sucking. "You help me with Magdalene," he commands in between teasing nibbles. "Help me make this place a true home for her—" At least he has insight into his current anti-child décor. "Do this for me, and I will ensure that you are sufficiently sprung."

My toes curl.

"And if I refuse?"

His hand slides boldly between my legs, and I inhale, my thoughts spinning. "You won't," he smugly surmises, *barely* grazing my piercing. "My money may not impress you, but I know what does. You've just had your first dose of the day," he reminds me as my face heats further. "I will keep you well supplied. As long as you help me. Anything else can be discussed at a later date. I just need you to promise me this."

I stroke his chest, more touched by his confession than I care to admit out loud. When the man engages in his limited pillow talk, my senses combust. But when he's open? Something in my heart starts to bleed, and I'm worried that it's not entirely a bad feeling.

"I'll help you," I tell him, smoothing my fingers across his rock-hard pec. "I'll help you with your daughter."

He captures my chin, tilting it so that our lips meet fiercely. I moan into the kiss, arching against him, frowning when he pulls back.

"What's wrong?"

"First, I need your help with something else," he tells me, brushing his lips across my jaw in a series of featherlight touches that make my eyelids flutter. "Something marginally less important, but still requiring urgent attention."

I frown, confused. "What?"

That grin. It's so quick and devastating in its prowess. A flash of white teeth paired with a hint of mischief in those dark eyes. I'm dumbstruck.

"Come." He stands, pulling me along with him even though we're both naked. My involuntary shiver must be what makes him take a detour to the closet where he snatches one of his shirts from its hanger and dresses me in it. "I think I prefer this to…"

He breaks off, his throat clenching, and I beam in triumph and finger the tip of his starched collar. On me, the shirt strains over my breasts, and I have a feeling he can see my nipples protruding against the material.

New sexy outfit idea? *Check, check, check.*

"Oh, Mr. Vadim. Are you saying that you *like* to see me in your clothing?" I twirl for his benefit and relish in his savoring moan.

"Witch!" He grabs my wrist and spins me around to face him. Ravenous, his eyes rake over me, settling on my chest. He can *definitely* see my nipples judging from his appreciative swallow. "I think I love you in my clothing," he confesses, his voice rasping.

And I'm more aware of my piercing than ever, hovering dangerously close to my clit. So on fire, it's nearly unbearable.

"But, you may be too distracting." He slides his fingers beneath my collar in search of the topmost button and swiftly undoes it. Then another. Another. Soon, the garment is hanging open, exposing my torso, and some of the heat in his gaze simmers to a liquid lust that makes me sway. "Much better," he declares before finding a shirt of his own.

I follow him from the room and into that infamous space the next door down. My breath catches as I spot the pillory, and my brain loses track of everything but the prospect of doing it again. For longer. With more spanking. More intensity. More.

"Finish your homework admirably, and I will reward you," Vadim says thickly as if reading my mind.

"Homework?"

"Furniture," he declares. "For her room..." Without explaining further, he crosses over to that corner of stacked boxes and easily lifts a massive one from the nearest row. He brings it to the center of the room and places it down. Wiping his hands, he nods to a section of the room I hadn't noticed until now.

"My laptop is there," he says, indicating a small, neatly arranged collection of items. A pillow. A folded blanket. A laptop. A stack of clothing. My throat constricts as I pad closer and recognize the small corner as where he must have stayed during his exile from the master bed—in addition to his study—though I suspect his laptop and briefcase saw much more use than the pillow and blanket did.

"You can use it to do your research," he adds.

Nodding, I grab the laptop and obediently bring it toward him as he opens a box with a silver knife. He logs me in and opens up a browser before returning back to his main task. I peek over his shoulder and watch on excitedly while he rummages through a carefully packed arrangement of black wood.

"Another toy?" I wonder, a thrill in my voice.

"Attend to your assignment, Ms. Connors," he scolds, eyeing me from over his shoulder. "And, I will attend to mine."

Challenge accepted. I hunker down with his laptop and try to decide where to begin. I don't feel the need to ask him for direction, at least. He wants me to help him prepare the house for Magda. Predictably, I do a cursory search for girl's bedroom ideas only to find myself distracted as Vadim rolls up the sleeves of his shirt and casually lifts massive piece of wood, after massive piece from the box and begins to assemble them using the white instruction manual as a guide.

The man has skill. He works methodically, utilizing his hands in a graceful display to manipulate the various pieces and screw or hammer them together. My cheeks flame as he looks up and catches me spying.

"Ten minutes in and you haven't spent millions? I'm disappointed, Ms. Connors," he chides playfully.

I scoff. "Watch me."

I return to the screen, peering through an endless array of furniture listings and design styles. I'm observing a promising pastel color scheme when something flashes across the screen. An email alert? I frown as I scan the subject heading.

"You speak Russian?" I ask, vaguely recognizing the unfamiliar shapes of the Cyrillic alphabet from a brief lesson on the Bolshevik revolution in high school.

"What?" Vadim looks up sharply, setting his tools aside. He grabs the laptop from me and quickly scans the contents of the email. Whatever he reads makes him curse, and he slams the computer shut, turning on his heel. "I'll be back," he says in a tone that warns me not to follow.

Seconds later, I hear his voice drift from the bedroom. He must be on a phone call. "You want to play peacemaker?" he demands in a scathing tone. "Keep your dog on his leash. I've restrained myself where he is concerned because *you* asked. I've gone to your dinners, and played your game, but if he dares to play his games with me, I'll end this war for good. I'm warning you both, Milton—" he pauses as if allowing the person on the other end to reply. Whatever they say makes him laugh. "It seems that someone's been digging around my holdings in Moscow," he adds. "Who else but Maxim? Unlike him, I've kept my enemies in check. How much more am I supposed to sacrifice to keep little Maxi sated? Rest assured, I'll give him a friendly warning to keep his distance. *Adieu.*"

He must hang up, because he's entering the room a heartbeat later, his expression haggard. Spotting me, he clenches his jaw and returns to his scattered tools.

"Change your mind?" he asks as he snatches up two long pieces of wood and secures them to a rectangular base. "You can still use my computer—"

"No," I say, still stunned by the ferocity I've just witnessed. It's like he flips in some ways, flicking between these two halves of his personality. My mind is burning with questions—what has his brother done now? But something inexplicable warns me from asking.

So I don't.

"I'm just reassessing," I say instead. "I think it might be better to make these purchases in person. Find something special. Do you even know what she likes? Dislikes?"

He looks down, his jaw tight. "There is a list in the documentation from her social worker," he admits.

"You've read it?"

He stares off into the distance and slowly nods.

"We'll look for things together, then," I suggest, rising to my feet. The real world lingers beyond this room, but I'm selfish. Childish, even. I'm desperate to extend this moment, and I cross over to him without a second's hesitation, looping my arms around his neck from behind. "Tomorrow we'll go out and buy some things for her in person. Do I still get my treat?"

He stiffens, but then cups my hips, and any previous tension eases. "Remember when, during your explicit proposal of your demands in exchange for a piercing, that you requested a swing?"

He makes it sound so harmless, but I squeal in utter debauched delight. It's a relatively effortless gesture on his part, but it betrays an intent that leaves me giddy—more debauched kink. My eyes trace the contours of the rectangular base, and I slowly begin to recognize the makings of a sexual swing set. Just for me.

"I love how you make my fantasies come true," I murmur near his ear.

He strokes down my hip, and I sense again that something unspoken is being transferred between us. Something hot and sensual that makes me back away.

"Let me be your assistant?" I ask as he turns to face me.

He smirks and directs me to a leather case containing silver tools. I perch beside it and hand him tools one by one at his request. I think he manages to work for a solid hour in peace before the pressure building between my legs becomes unbearable. Being with him is forcing me to rethink all the turn-ons I'd had before now.

A man wearing only a dress shirt, screwing pieces of a sex swing together? *Check.*

Said man glancing at me every few seconds with hooded, lusty eyes? *Double check.*

And when he stands and rakes his fingers through a mane of curls glistening with sweat, I shrug off my own shirt and sidle up to him, easing a silver wrench from his grasp.

"I want a demonstration," I murmur, stroking my fingers along the partially built swing. Then I inch the same hand around to his abdomen and boldly stroke downward. "A taste of all the dirty things you plan to do to me on it?"

In exasperation, he turns to me and captures my chin, his grin dangerous. "I'll never finish at this rate," he says, eyeing my front.

I shamelessly display myself for him and cup one of my breasts, thumbing the nipple. "You could always say no," I remind him.

His eyes narrow as if he's processing the idea. The next second, he's stepping into me, his mouth finding mine, his hands gripping my hips. One harsh tug brings my pelvis against his.

I take that response as a yes.

CHAPTER FIVE

I wake up dazed, lying on a hard surface. The floor? Beside me rests a warm, tempting body that I greedily nestle against even as my eyes open and blink to adjust to the dim light. *Oh.* I vaguely recognize the budding sex room, complete with the partially-built swing looming above.

And beside me is Vadim, his cheek resting on the open manual and my heart practically melts. No man has ever looked sexier and I can't resist stroking my fingers along his jaw until he opens his eyes.

"Your playground will take months to achieve at this rate," he says tiredly. I arch into him as his arms encircle me, drawing me closer.

"Good," I say with absolutely no regret. "In the meantime, we can build one for Magda—but I promise I won't strip naked while you work on *her* swing set."

He chuckles at that, sounding skeptical. "When do you want to begin your search, oh expert?"

I glance at the gray light coming in through the window and wiggle away from him, climbing to my feet. "Now."

I help him up and lead him into the shower where I risk a small delay to reward him for indulging me. Together we dress quickly —him in a plain black suit and I settle on a dress in a matching color—and, after a quick breakfast, we take the sports car into the city.

I lean into him, stroking his arm while my brain plays some frantic warning about my own boundaries. My own deadline. My own red lines—I told him this would end soon. After Magda is settled, I need to leave. It will be best for everyone.

"Having second thoughts?" Vadim asks as I pull away from him and focus my attention on the window nearest me.

"H-Huh?" I look over, but he doesn't appear anywhere near as distraught about us ending this as one might assume.

"I assure you that I am not a good shopping companion," he confesses. "Are you sure you can't manage alone?"

Oh. I brush my fingers along his forearm and squeeze the rock-hard muscle lurking beneath. "I need your strength," I insist. "I plan to put your skills as a handyman to use."

"Handy, you say…" His upper lip quirks as he scans the road. "There are people I can hire for that."

"No." I marvel at the authority my own voice packs. "I want *you* to do it. Some things we can make exceptions for, but you should have a hand in this."

He doesn't respond but his eyes take on that far-away darkness. Desperate to change the subject, I lean down and fish through his briefcase until I find a blue folder containing a stack of neatly printed documents. I can tell even as I spread them over my lap that they have been well-perused before me. The edges are dented from what I suspect were a pair of slim fingers flipping through them over and over. Still, I feign ignorance as I spot a small but detailed list.

"She likes blue," I read, awed by that preference she unknowingly shares with the man beside me. "She enjoys reading. She likes to play chess. She enjoys—"

"Swimming," Vadim finishes before I can. "Playing in the park. Boats. Her favorite food is buttered toast. She also likes horses." He speaks with such a confidence that I don't even have to glance at the paper to know he's memorized them by heart.

And the fact that his home contains both a swimming pool and a stable, as well as a boathouse takes on a new meaning. One that leaves me stunned.

"*That's* why you picked that house," I say, returning the papers to the briefcase. "I thought you wanted to be a dick to your brother, but it was for her."

His lips contort into a small, beautiful smile that reveals just how exhausted he is. How many nights has he lost worrying about this? Far too many I suspect.

"I cannot be faulted if Maxim also has an interest in child friendly real-estate. Not to mention that I've owned…" He trails off, his jaw tight. "Contrary to Maxim's egotistical view, my life does not entirely revolve around spiting him."

I recall the phone conversation I overheard last night, more disturbed than before. What trouble might be building between the brothers now?

Today probably isn't the best time to dig for answers on that subject, however.

"It's a beautiful house," I say, gently steering the topic to safer waters. "But together, we'll make it perfect for her. I promise." I interlink my fingers with his free hand, squeezing tight. He risks taking his eyes from the road just long enough to eye our clasped hands.

"Together…" He says the word as though it's a novel concept. One he's never applied to his life before and again I seethe in jealousy at whichever potential wife he may have picked. No one will help him like I will.

But then you'll leave him, a part of me snipes. *You plan on skipping out as soon as you can, you heartless bitch.*

"Have you decided where to attack first, Ms. General?" Vadim wonders once we reach the city proper.

I latch onto the distraction and tap my chin, humming thoughtfully. "No. But I did find a custom boutique online. Everything they sell looks insanely expensive yet beautifully crafted. Let's start there."

He chuckles. "Let's see if you can reach my expectations. With my accounts at your mercy, I should be nearing bankruptcy by the evening's end. I hope you won't disappoint."

"You're on," I declare, with upmost confidence.

But something tells me that the stakes of this little venture may result in more than just his finances being at risk. Like my resolve for one.

And my boundaries, too.

AFTER A MORNING SPENT SHOPPING, we have lunch and then take a detour to a high-rise that I recognize as one of his offices. Eingel Industries reads the name emblazoned on the corridors as he leads me inside.

"I need to grab some legal documents," he tells me. "I'll be just a moment."

And yet, he didn't have me wait in the car or come here himself. Could this be a reclusive billionaire's attempt at transparency? My heart flutters, unsure of how to accept this deliberate turn of events.

As a good thing, I decide.

"I'll wait out here," I suggest, spotting a pair of glass doors that appear to lead into an enclosed courtyard. Vadim nods and sets off while I venture out into a small, beautiful garden brimming with carefully cultivated bushes and flower beds. A bubbling fountain ties the peaceful scenery together but when I spy a golden plaque my heart constricts as I read the simple phrase inscribed on it—*Hiram Gorgoshev Memorial Garden.*

A family member of his? Given what little he's revealed about his past, I'm not even sure if I should risk asking.

I'm instantly aware the second he steps out to join me. It's as if the entire atmosphere shifts. Thickens. Mellows.

A lazy smile is already playing on my lips even before I feel his hands on my waist as he comes up behind me. "My accounts are settled," he murmurs against the nape of my neck. "You may continue to spend as you please."

My brain reels at that, considering that—together, based mainly on his input—we've already spent a small fortune on enough furniture and small knick knacks to please any seven-year-old.

"I'll turn you into a shopaholic yet," I declare, spinning around to face him. He looks so freaking pretty in the pale, overcast daylight. Like a fallen angel finally remembering to unfurl his wings after an eternity of damnation. Hopeful.

I hate myself for daring to mention, "This garden… It's beautiful."

He shoots me an odd look, an eyebrow raised. "Do you think she'd want one like it?" Before I can reply he slips an arm around my shoulders and steers me back through the building, out to the car.

"A garden would be a nice touch," I say, letting the subject drop.

As we pull away from the building, his eyes linger on it, and for a split second, his expression slips. Raw pain distorts his features and I want to kick myself for ever bringing up the subject.

Whoever Hiram Gorgoshev was to him, I suspect he doesn't think on him with quite the same hostility he utilizes toward his brother or his past.

But he isn't ready to talk about him either, and I can't help but wonder why.

CHAPTER SIX

"A little to the left," I command while leaning against a wall of newly purchased pillows, all still wrapped within their plastic packaging. Before me stands Vadim, musing over the correct placement for a scenic portrait.

"Here?" he asks, moving the ivory frame slightly to the left.

"Maybe to the right," I say, but I'm admittedly not staring at the painting but something far more enticing just a few feet below. I'm caught when he turns around and catches me gawking.

"Are you referring to the painting or my ass?"

"Both," I confess sheepishly. "You're sexy when in interior designer mode—the room looks beautiful."

And it should—the combined effort of over twenty hours of work, building and painting with a night spent sleeping on the floor to boot. The space he had chosen for Magda was originally beautiful with a perfect view of the water and the surrounding property—though utterly bare. At its core were the basics for a girl's dream bedroom, however. A bay window, complete with a window seat, conjures the image of a father reading bedtime stories, and the bed we picked out is made of a luxurious pale wood.

"I would have died for a room like this," I tell him, meaning every word.

"Would you have?" A grin ignites his wary expression, battling the exhaustion and streaks of baby blue paint still speckling his cheeks. I suck in a breath, horrified. My sore piercing—thank God it isn't infected or damaged despite my throwing the healing instructions to the wind—throbs in a delicious tempo in tune to my racing heartbeat. "You're going to rock the single father trope."

"Single?" He tilts his head, stroking his chin with fingers reddened from assembling furniture for hours on end. Something feral seeps into his gaze, eating away at the playful demeanor until… God, he looks too damn serious.

I jump as he pivots, setting the picture aside, and advances toward me, his gaze crackling. The faster I move, the wider his strides become until he's gained on me. With the tip of his finger, he tilts my chin back, forcing eye contact.

"Single is not something I foresee for myself," he murmurs, stroking my jaw in a devastating, toe-curling swipe. "Not anymore."

"Haha." I inhale sharply and take a small step back. "Planning on another wife so soon? At least let us have our fake divorce first," I say, attempting a joke. It falls flat—my voice is a hoarse whisper, and Vadim doesn't laugh.

"Not quite…" He advances again, ruthlessly pinning me against the wall, until I have no choice but to quiver against him. His gaze is too damn intense, demanding in a way that makes my hips arch despite my protests, my pulse thready.

"No new wife. No new woman—" his sly, devious grin makes me exhale sharply, contrasting with the way he sweeps his touch down to my throat, each fingertip radiating possession. All the while, his gaze remains honed, sharper than ever. Determined. "I think I have denied myself of happiness for too long. I think I'd like to renegotiate our options."

"N-No." I shake my head, attempting to turn away. "I told you. This won't work—"

"You did." He captures my cheek against his palm, urging me to face him again. "But I suggest we renegotiate those terms. In fact… I insist upon it."

"No!" I sound exasperated, and again I try to escape from around him—but he shifts to block me at every turn.

"Vadim." My heartbeat falters as I brace my hand over his chest. "Please don't," I croak. "Please. I don't want to ruin this."

He blinks, and just like that, he flips his internal switch. He's neutral again, the fire gone. All I sense from him now is ice-cold calm. "As you wish."

He returns to the wall and picks up the frame, relentlessly hammering it into place within seconds. I watch him, wary for reasons I can't explain. His insistence isn't what unnerves me. It's my own—and fear of things not working out isn't what makes me want to run far in the opposite direction. No… I find myself stroking the fake ring on my finger as I grapple with the truth— I'm terrified by how good things *could* be. So good. And I don't know if I can face the disappointment if that fantasy never comes to fruition.

My time with Jim taught me that relationships, for the most part, *always* fall apart.

I'm so lost within myself that I barely notice when Vadim leaves the room for good. It isn't until I find myself searching for him that I finally register his absence. Alone, I stand and pace the room, marveling at the small touches that his money alone couldn't buy.

For one, he mixed two shades of blue to find the perfect hue to accent the wall above her bed. He found trinkets and books to fill her shelves, picked out without my input. Each detail reveals the depth of a devotion I doubt even he is truly aware of.

He wants his daughter with him. He craves her happiness. And I can't come in between them before they even have the chance to connect.

Right?

To distract myself from pondering the answer, I gather up the loose pieces of trash strewn across the room. Then I unwrap the pillows and dress them in the crisp, baby blue sheets we picked out together at a boutique downtown. I adorn the bed with them and add a matching comforter and ivory woven throw blanket.

All in all, it's a room any little girl would love.

Left with nothing else to do, I have no choice but to face the world beyond this room. And the conversation I sense lies in wait the second I do. Warily, I creep down the hall toward the bedroom. There, I find Vadim standing in the center of the space, his face in his hands, his back to me. Seeing him in torment makes me ache in ways I never have. Like my heart is on fire, and only his nearness can put it out. To do so, I'll risk bending my own rules, just a little. I can't help it.

"Let's forget what we said," I suggest, approaching him. "I don't want to fight. I don't—"

He spins around, capturing my wrists, drawing me close. A shudder runs through me as our lips connect, tongues meeting hesitantly. Closing my eyes, I sink into the kiss, letting him overpower me with forceful, deep strokes. Too forceful. Devouring. I'm dizzy when he pulls back, and I blink my eyes open, gasping for breath.

He's flipped that internal switch again, suddenly ablaze with an array of emotions too obscure to name outright.

"You've ruined everything," he tells me, his eyes darker than ever. Furious. Resigned. Terrifying. As I stiffen, he caresses my jaw, his expression pained. "You give me a taste of what it could be like... How could I not want more?"

"Huh?"

He leans in without explanation, taking my mouth with a ferocity that leaves me breathless. I cling to him, buffeted back as he surges forward. Without warning, he shoves me down, forcing me onto my back.

I look up at him, dazed, my throat tightening as he reaches for his pants, easily tugging them open. Fire shoots through me, and my brain goes blank as my legs spread apart. Only a frantic warning at the back of my mind makes me gasp out, "Wait—"

"You feel it, don't you?" he inquires with that smug confidence as he rips his pants down his legs and frees his cock from the boxers beneath. My teeth seize my bottom lip at the sight. He's erect, his piercing gleaming, precum wetting the pulsating crown.

So beautiful.

And *dangerous*. I recognize that look in his eye. That cold, calculating expression. The same one he sported after tormenting me with the silver toy and locking me in the pillory.

Punishing.

"You feel it," he repeats too quickly for my sluggish brain to keep up. "This…rightness. Don't you?"

I nod—anything to keep him pleasuring himself with those firm, confident strokes. Only belatedly do I register his words and the husky way he delivered them. Like a prayer. Something sacred he doesn't confess lightly.

Only in worship. Reverence. Desperation.

"Vadim…" My brain swims as I try to sit up and muster my tongue into forming some semblance of coherence. "We need to talk about this—"

He moves, cutting me off as he leans over me, bringing his pelvis dangerously close to the heat building between my legs. I writhe shamelessly, forgetting my train of thought all over again. But it's important, I think. Something about boundaries. Reinforcing them. And if I don't…

Things will go way too far.

"No relationship," I insist as I arch my hips to meet his anyway. But he pulls back. My wrists are in his grasp before I know it. He spreads them apart, forcing my arms above my head. Suddenly, a firm pressure replaces his grip over my left wrist, and I hear a subtle snap! Dazed, I crane my neck back and find a strap of leather tethering that arm to the bed.

"W-What are you—"

Snap! My other wrist is immobile as well, impossible to move.

Alarmed, I look down, too stunned to fully process my predicament. Manacled again? "Vadim…"

He shifts his weight, settling between my legs, but his eyes hold my attention this time, even as my body radiates with his nearness. He's never looked clearer, more intense. Intent. Like a dog insistent on having his bone, no matter the cost.

"So beautiful," he praises, sweeping his gaze along the length of me. I nearly jump out of my skin as he strokes his thumb down my chest. Even through the fabric of another one of his borrowed shirts, my skin ignites. "I had everything planned, but you."

I mull over that calculating term. *Planned?* Desperate to regain my focus, I experimentally tug my arms.

"You won't get free," he tells me as he stands, leaving a gaping absence where his heat used to be. "They are custom made from a craftsman in Germany. Specifically designed for your measurements. I can assure you that both are of the highest quality and designed to be tamper-proof."

I frown as my gaze fixates on his cock, my body quivering. "Why tie me up?"

His smile…

It steals my breath in a startled gasp as an ominous pressure begins to build in my belly. Lust, fed by *this* despite my own insistence. Aware of every tendril of heat, a devious gleam sets his dark eyes alight, making them glow. He's more beautiful than ever.

"I aim to convince you to change your mind," he says. "I respect your concerns. I do. But I do not think I should let you cling to them without hearing my perspective."

He releases his cock, and I bite back a groan. What an amazing perspective.

Snap out of it, Tiffy! Sex isn't the only defining factor of a relationship. If it were, we'd be golden. But there's so much more.

"I can't be a mother," I tell him, jumping right to the heart of the matter. "Helping you keep her is as far as I can go. No more. I can't. You know why. Please respect that."

His expression falls flat, and it's a double-edged sword. Some of the lust churning my thoughts to mush dissipates—but in return, guilt descends like a sucker punch. The man has me tied to a bed, but the idea of disappointing him alarms me more than anything else. Maybe because he's being open for once, hiding nothing from me.

Not even his pain.

"I'm sorry," I whisper.

He turns away, shielding his expression, and I strain my binds, my legs flailing.

"Wait! Don't go!"

He leaves anyway, slipping through the doorway without a second glance. Before I can even panic, he's back, and in his hands is an object that makes my eyes go wide.

And my stomach drops right through the floor.

"No," I whisper, in panicked horror. Flailing, I strain at my binds to no avail, my voice rising in pitch. "No… Don't."

Heedless of my pleas, he stalks forward, brandishing the object that makes me gasp, partly terrified, partly…excited. It's a silver dildo, similar to the remote-controlled one. But larger. Longer. Thicker.

I clamp my knees together as he advances toward the bed, shaking my head.

"No. No. Vadim!"

The bastard doesn't wrench my legs apart like a brute. He caresses me instead, smoothing his fingers up and down my hip, barely touching my skin. Over and over. The gentleness with which he does so is such a startling contrast to the intent etched within his hungry features that my brain doesn't know how to process it. A part of me lurches into his touch while the other fixates on that damn silver toy.

"I won't hurt you," he swears, his voice a persistent, soothing hum. "I will never hurt you."

And I believe him, even as he lowers that toy between my legs.

"Look at me," he commands. When I do, I almost can't breathe at the intensity I find in his gaze. He eyes me like I'm something more than just beautiful. Cherished. Desired. My thoughts spin again, threatening to scatter.

But when a cool, firmness nudges my lower lips, I balk.

"Vadim, please…"

Pressure. Pressure. Thick, filling pressure. Shock robs me of my voice as my head rears back. Deep down, I know that he's using the toy, easing it inside me bit by bit.

"So beautiful," I hear him grate as my muscles relax to adjust. "So wet for me. Trust me, beautiful. I will never hurt you."

Because he wants to kill me instead.

This toy is deadly. I can sense the subtle differences from the last one the second he breaches me with the rounded tip. After a few days, the shape and feel of his cock are etched into my brain. How it stretches me pleasurably. The friction he can achieve with just one stroke.

And this toy…

It's *him.* In almost every fucking way.

"Yes," he says in response to my puzzled expression. Gently, he smooths the hair from my face and leans over me, trailing his lips along my sweat-slick forehead. "Another custom request," he adds near my ear. "You ask for pleasure, I aim to deliver."

He shoves his hand—driving in the toy in the process—and my brain goes on hiatus. Too much. Too fast. My eyes roll, my breaths shallow as my body conforms to the foreign object— familiar, yet different. Nothing in the world could ever serve as a substitute for him, and in so many ways, the toy feels worse. The pressure only heightens the lust throbbing between my legs. My inner muscles clench in vain, demanding the real thing. It's sadistic.

It's torture, beyond kink.

It's exquisite.

"D-Devil," I whisper as my senses reassemble, and I realize his intent. Drive me insane.

"Angel," he praises, still petting my dampening hair. "So beautiful. Tell me you'll stay with me. That I can give you what you need, *oui?*"

"No," I counter forcefully as my eyelids flutter—but he nudges the toy just enough to press against my gripping muscles, sowing incredible friction. I have to gulp at the air to survive the rippling contractions. "Can't…"

"You can," he insists, maddeningly calm. "In a few days, you've made me rethink my entire life's trajectory. I think you can readjust your stubborn beliefs. Tell me you will."

But I have. I've thought of what life could be with him, even playing house with a child who doesn't even know he exists. It sounds sick on paper. In reality? It could be so very good, and I'm terrified by just how appealing it seems.

Because every sense in my brain is telling me that nothing could ever be that good. Run away. Disengage. Kill that hope now before it festers.

"You belong with me." His voice. It's sin, falling into a deep, smooth cadence that renders me gasping. "I told you once to ask yourself… Would I ever let you go? From the moment you leaped on my cock as though it were a treat, I knew you were mine. You *will* be mine."

He sounds mad. Too serious. This isn't a game anymore.

Unease rises up to combat the pleasure swirling around my brain. "V-Vadim, please—" I cry out. At the back of my mind, I realize why—he shoved the toy in deeper.

"I never knew sex could be like this," he says, sounding miles away, and yet at the same time, his voice resonates through my brain as if implanted there. "More," he adds hoarsely. "I never knew. You think I'd let you go so easily?" He laughs as my eyes flutter to him, and I barely catch a devious grin before he thrusts the toy again. Deeper. Harder.

My back arches, jerking off the mattress. "Vadim!"

"I never knew it could be like this with another person," he adds, his voice rasping, eyes heavy-lidded. "Tell me, do you deny it?"

"Yes," I croak, only to gasp as he wrenches the dildo free.

"You don't feel the same?" he wonders, his tone mocking. "Should I leave you like this?"

I shudder at the horror. "No! No!"

"Then tell me…have you ever felt this with anyone else? This pleasure?"

The toy returns, easing inside of me, and my eyes roll at the sensation.

"No," I murmur before I can bite the word back.

"Tell me how good it feels."

He stills again, and it's like my body takes on a will of its own. My hips sway, seeking out more pressure. More depth.

"Tell me," he insists, threatening to pull back.

"G-Good!" I whimper in relief as he slams the toy home. The pleasure hits like a wave. My brain goes blank, and I hear my mewling cries echoing off the walls. "So good."

"Damn, you're beautiful," he says thickly, and I moan in response. "So beautiful. So wet for me. Do you ache for me?"

I nearly scream as he jerks the toy. "Yes."

And it's true. I'm throbbing in a way that I never have. On fire.

"Tell me how badly."

All I can do is whimper. "Please—"

"Tell me."

"I need you. I need you."

"Fuck, you're incredible." I realize somewhere within the shambles of my brain that it's the first time I've heard him curse like this. Truly unrestrained. Wild. A creature unleashed from his own constraints. "Look at me, beautiful."

With difficultly, I refocus on him, and my heart stalls. He looks magnetic. Powerful. Like a predator, looming above dying prey. "Tell me... Tell me you need me. Say it—"

"I need you," I croak, shameless. "Please."

"Tell me I can have you." He leans down, brushing his lips against my quivering throat. "Tell me I deserve you."

My brain reels at his tone. Guttural. Broken. Teasing aside, this is far beyond sex. Too far.

"Vadim—"

He nips, rendering me silent. "Say it. I deserve you. I... I am *owed* you. No one can take you from me. Not him. Not God. No one."

"Vadim, listen—"

A scream rips away any other coherent words I might say. My spine arches off the bed as ecstasy explodes through my body. Buzzing. Persistent vibration...

The toy is electric, and he's just turned it on.

"Stay with me," he urges, his tone radiating authority. "Stay with me, beautiful. Look at me."

My eyes stream, throat rasping as I meet his gaze. He looks so open in this moment. So raw—and the intensity building within me only strengthens. A brutal orgasm is looming, one so devastating I almost fear it.

"I will have you," Vadim swears. He withdraws the toy, setting it aside, and I moan wordlessly as he settles over me, his cock throbbing against my inner thigh. "I will keep you. I will own you. Say that you're mine."

He thrusts in so deep I think I lose consciousness. When my senses return, I'm gasping, dizzy and dazed, clawing at the sheets as he slams inside of me.

I cry out his name as my body convulses over and over. He's steel, pulsating against my inner walls. And yet, as stern as ever, his voice drips into my ear, murmured like a prayer. "Come for me, beautiful. So wet. So perfect. Tell me you need this. You need *me*."

I comply in whimpers and groans, too far gone to speak logically. As he moves, I lose track of time and space. Of how many times I come.

It's pleasure beyond any physical understanding. I'm drugged, overwhelmed, drowning in him. But even in my dazed, broken brain, I take note of when he groans, his throat cording, hands grasping my hips.

He throws his head back, groaning my name as his release floods me in fiery waves.

And I know that my attempts at putting distance between us were pathetic, pitiful lies. Much like our very first meeting, I was never in control.

Not really.

He's always had an alternate plan, one I suspect I'm barely aware of even now. All I can do is surrender to the chaos and try to swim against the current.

Or drown.

"You are *mine*," he declares, collapsing against me. "And I will take what I am owed..."

CHAPTER SEVEN

"Did I hurt you?" Vadim asks, his voice a low rasp.

I'm in his arms, too weak to move. At some point, he must have released me from the manacles because my arms are free, trembling at my sides. With what little strength I can muster, I shake my head and rest my cheek against his shoulder.

"No," I tell him as he strokes my back with so much gentleness it leaves me reeling. "No, you didn't hurt me."

"I'm sorry," he adds, brushing his lips across my damp forehead. He doesn't say for what. For sexual torture? For pushing my fragile boundaries to their limits? For a part of his plan, I'm woefully unaware of?

"I do want you," I croak, letting my eyes shut as exhaustion barrels through me, mixed with guilt and regret. All of it creates a tumult so vast, the only way through it is to just talk. "I do. I'm just afraid. I don't want to disappoint you or *be* disappointed. I've been through too damn much… I can't be disappointed."

He laughs so deeply that I force myself to open my eyes merely to see his face. He's eyeing the ceiling, his lips contorted into a tired grin.

"I've never had a relationship, so perhaps that fear isn't entirely misplaced…"

"Never?" I can't hide my skepticism. I'm practically in a coma after a bout of ruthless, vicious sex. Does he really expect me to believe that no other woman has experienced this with him?

No, I realize with growing awe. He doesn't care either way, because it's the truth. A rare hint of vulnerability shapes his expression, betraying just how uneasy he is at opening up to me. Which further reinforces the gravity of the fact that he's doing so at all.

"What did you call me?" he wonders, grimacing at the memory. "Mean? I call it prudent. Most people don't seek more from me than what they want in the moment. What they can gain. My brother sees me as a burden. To Ena, I am a partner. Even Milton sees me as a scared little boy he's sworn to protect. As for women? I've never experienced more than sex."

"Their loss," I rasp, letting my face fall against his chest, utterly spent. But a part of me bristles at his boasts. Someone like him —so used to using manipulation as a tool—might see those relationships in such stark terms. But a partnership without true concern doesn't result in someone stocking the fridge of their employer just to ensure they eat. And Milton… I saw how he intervened between him and his brother. Someone who didn't care wouldn't do that. Could a man be so blind as to the genuine love of those around him? Woe to any woman who dared to broach the topic. "I think I should be pleased to be the recipient of your pent-up lust," I add, changing the subject to safer waters.

"Thirty-one years of it," he declares, sliding his hand down my back. "Why shouldn't I demand more? I am tired of waiting for my turn."

His turn?

"You make me explore things I never thought possible," he adds with a subtle hint of inflection that makes me quiver. "I *will* break you down… I can be persistent when it comes to that which I desire. You have been warned."

Does he truly mean that? My aching body shivers at the possibilities. I could cry at the potential, and yet my toes still curl, ravenous for more.

"I love being with you," I confess, lulled by the thrum of his heartbeat. "I just don't want to hurt you."

"You hurt me?" He laughs again, this sound more beautiful than the first. "I think I can suffer whatever pain you can dish out, as long as you perform your unique way of currying favor afterward."

"Ah." I lift my lips, pleased that he seems to enjoy my "ways" as much as I do. "And just to think, a few days ago, I had to fight you to let me suck your cock."

"A foolish man, then," he concedes. "Such a fool. But he is thankfully in the past. Stay with me, and I will learn plenty of ways to both pleasure you and explore the use of your mouth."

He pulls me closer, holding me so tight it's just to the point of painful. For some reason, it's easier to write off his words as boasts made in the heat of the moment. Nothing more. Even as his gaze burns with searing intensity…

He's bluffing.

"Promise?" I say, testing that assumption despite my better judgment.

"I will," he declares as if to shatter that hope. "No promise necessary."

I WAKE up to the sensation of peace, unlike any other. One so deep and so encompassing that I assume I'm dreaming at first. No one's arms could possibly feel this safe. This warm. This comforting.

I open my eyes, expecting a fantasy realm of unicorns and ponies and other fantastical dreamworld things. Instead, I find a man so beautiful he can't be real. My heart despairs until he opens his dark eyes, and his expression matches mine. Fearful with diminishing hope. There's no way this can be real.

I snuggle into him, attempting to extend this moment for as long as I can only for him to stiffen. Gradually, his frown softens, his eyes losing their unease. I shiver as his fingers part my hair, smoothing through the strands as he sighs, utterly relaxed.

This may not be a dream, after all.

"Morning."

I moan at the sound of his voice, husky with sleep. "Morning," I whisper in response.

So yes, this is real. Vadim, holding me against him, our bodies still slick with sweat, the bedsheets twisted around us. Pale dawn light bathes his skin in a soft glow, making him seem more ethereal than ever. My beautiful, tormented angel so convinced he doesn't deserve happiness.

He has to take it.

All of last night comes crashing back in one go. My ultimatum. His sensual, torturous response. Something in my expression must change because he stiffens, betraying breathtaking concern. Horror, even.

And I do nothing to reassure him. Slowly, I brace my hand against his chest and push back, wincing as my body throbs with a mixture of lingering lust and bone-shattering exhaustion.

"I'll never forgive you," I tell him, my voice breaking. "Never."

His throat constricts as he reaches for me, stroking my cheek. "I'm sorry. Are you in pain?"

I snatch his hand, wrenching it from my face. Then I manipulate the digits until the longest finger is extended, and I eagerly brush it with my lips, stroking my tongue across the tip. He looks horribly confused, this beautiful man, torn between arousal and alarm.

I deign to put him out of his misery and suck on the very tip of his finger just once.

"How dare you keep that toy all to yourself," I scold him, still too weak to put real effort into my mocking tone. "I'm starting to think I should demand you come clean about all of your new custom goodies."

He chuckles and gingerly slips his finger from my lips, drawing me closer. "I plan to keep you well satisfied on the real thing," he says, and sure enough, I sense him hardening against my belly. "That substitute shall only be deployed in emergencies."

"You see my potential leaving as an emergency?" I question, my voice soft.

He brushes my jaw, his lips firmly closed. "You're shaking," he finally declares, eyeing the length of me with a frown. "It seems another round of pampering is in order."

He shrugs the sheets from his body and stands. A heartbeat later, I'm in his arms as he heads for the bathroom. When we pass the window, I eye the morning sky and remember our unofficial deadline.

"Today is the last day before she comes," I declare. "I guess my playground will have to go under lock and key."

If he hears me, he doesn't respond. Instead, he drapes me carefully over the bench in the shower and proceeds to clean me off with more care than should be possible. After my few relationships—mainly with Jim—it blows my mind that someone can treat another person with such reverence. I feel like an idol worshipped by him. Revered by him.

And for a second, I can forget my rules—just for a second.

Determined, he bathes every inch of me with utmost gentleness. I'm riveted just watching him inspect me, awed by every part of me.

"You make me feel so beautiful," I murmur as he wipes the lather from my limbs and bundles me in a towel. "I love the way you—"

"My beauty, so full of compliments," he says while carrying me back into the bedroom. "You're inflating my ego. I've spent years fighting to keep it in check."

Rebelliously, I reach up, brushing my fingers along his jaw. "You deserve praise," I say, meaning every word. Perhaps that suspicion is what drives him to doubt the motives of those around him, even if they obviously care. "I give you permission to be as cocky as you want."

He makes a thoughtful sound in his throat as he settles me on the bed. He switched out the sheets, I realize, replacing them with a fresh set. "Cocky enough to think I can claim you?" he counters.

I sway as our gazes connect. It should be illegal for someone to look so…ravenous. And yet in the same breath, utterly restrained—all that tension tethered to a hair-trigger.

"Tell me you want me," I whisper, toying with that dangerous, fragile line.

With a feral expression, he snaps it. "I *crave* you."

To prove it, he leans down, making me feel so small in his massive shadow. Our lips meet, teeth gnashing with the ferocity. It isn't long before I'm beneath him, writhing for the pleasure only he can provide.

"Vadim, please—"

He slams into me before I can even finish voicing the plea. I hum in ecstasy, grasping for any part of him I can reach. My nails pierce the flesh of his forearms, but he moves, capturing both my wrists and pinning them flat to the bed.

Will he shackle me again? My heartbeat picks up at the prospect, but he merely entwines our fingers as our gazes reconnect. Somehow this tethering is more intimate. I feel even more helpless, rendered with no protection from the emotions spilling between us with every thrust. I grip him in return so tightly my hands shake.

My eyes threaten to roll as he rocks into me, taking me with a skill that dissolves every coherent thought, leaving only heat behind. Desire.

Panting, he brings his mouth near my ear, rasping, "You are mine."

I come around him, gasping his name.

And I let myself toy with the idea that his ownership may not be such a bad thing…

My list be damned.

CHAPTER EIGHT

We spend most of the morning in bed before finally venturing downstairs to eat one of Ena's frozen meals. Afterward, we put the finishing touches on Magda's room, hanging the final remaining pictures and arranging her blankets.

Just after midnight, we wind up in bed, our limbs entwined. I drift off cocooned in his arms, but the second I wake up, I know that everything has changed.

It's as if the air has become tinged with some unfamiliar scent, shifting the careful dynamic between us. Vadim rises from the bed without a word, his back to me, his fingers tearing through his hair. I roll onto my side and watch him, my heart swelling with too many emotions to decipher.

Today is the day everything between us changes. For better or for worse?

"We should get dressed," he says, his tone too neutral to give me an inkling either way.

He enters the closet and begins rummaging through the hanging clothing.

"The blue one," I tell him. "With the tie your brother brought you."

He shoots me an odd look, but as I crane my neck and sit upright, I see that he's complied, tugging on the navy suit with a black dress shirt.

I stand and follow him, stretching my sore limbs.

"The emerald dress," he tells me as I start to appraise my options. "With the cream jacket."

"An interesting color profile, Mr. Gorgoshev," I remark while I pick out the items in question. Once fully dressed, I eye myself and sigh in resignation.

Not only is the man sexy as hell, but he has an eye for fashion to match.

"I look like a very respectable fake wife," I say, surprised by the overall effect.

He comes to stand beside me, his expression approving. "Thank you for doing this for me," he says, leaning in to press his lips against my forehead. "I promise to find a safe place to reassemble your playground so that you may enjoy it fully."

I practically melt, and only the faint reminder at the back of my skull keeps me from trying to strip him naked—Magda.

Together, we enter the hallway, but as Vadim ventures downstairs, I take a detour to the next door over and peek inside. Sure enough, all of my charming apparatuses have vanished, leaving the room starkly bare. Surprisingly, I'm not too heartbroken as I descend the steps and enter the kitchen.

While we wait, I force feed Vadim a croissant, and I'm in the middle of goading him into drinking a glass of orange juice when a knock sounds at the front door.

He doesn't move. I'm the one who has to stand first and take his hand, leading the way to the front door. My heart pounds as I reach for the doorknob, only to have Vadim beat me to it. Gradually, he pulls the door open, revealing a smiling Ms. Anderson.

And beside her, is a little girl who looks as though she'd rather be anywhere else.

"Good morning!" Ms. Anderson beams and ushers the girl beside her inside. "I hope we aren't too early."

"N-No." Vadim shakes his head. Then he turns his attention to a small gray suitcase resting on the paved walkway. "Is that all of your things?"

Magda meets his gaze without flinching, her blue gaze electric. "The decent things," she says in that lilting voice. She steps forward, examining the foyer with an unreadable expression. God, the parallels between her and the man beside her mount up by the second.

The intensity of their gaze. The way they move, holding themselves with utmost confidence. Even their distaste, visible in how they purse their lips, their eyes narrowing.

"This is where I'm going to live now?" she asks.

"Of course, honey." Ms. Anderson chuckles nervously while Vadim grabs the suitcase, bringing it inside. "We...we talked about this, remember? Mr. Vadim and Ms. Tiffany are your new placement."

"Hmph." Magda turns her gaze to me, her arms crossed. She's carrying something crushed to her chest. White. Small. It isn't until she turns that I recognize the object from a different angle —an ivory teddy bear. Only…

"That's an interesting toy," I croak. No wonder the Robinsons were so disturbed.

Magda looks down while Ms. Anderson's cheeks promptly turn ten shades redder.

"His name is It," the girl declares, brandishing the bear by its head. A head that looks as though it's been ripped off at one point, only to be crudely sewn back on with a series of stitches in garishly red thread. "I don't really like him."

"Yes, well, Magda is very creative," Ms. Anderson explains with a nervous laugh. "Especially when it comes to her toys."

"Ah… Creative." I swallow hard and cut my gaze to Vadim. His expression is more guarded than ever.

"Well, I have my morning free," Ms. Anderson says quickly. "I would love to stay and help Magda get settled. I—" Frowning, she reaches into her briefcase as a musical sound begins to chime. A cell phone apparently. Pressing it to her ear, she says, "This is Angela. Oh, really? Now? But… No, I can be there—" she hangs up, frowning. "I'm so sorry. I planned on staying, but I just received an emergency call to attend to another case. Do you think you'll be fine if…"

"Yes," Vadim says hoarsely. "We'll be fine."

If she's convinced by his tone, Ms. Anderson's wary grin doesn't reveal much either way. With a small smile shaping her lips, she stoops down beside Magda and shakes her hand. "Be good. You all have my number if you need it. Even you, Mags."

"I won't be needing it," Magda says with steely confidence. Her eyes continue to skim around the room as if taking stock of every single tile in the flooring and divot in the wallpaper.

"Well, goodbye." Ms. Anderson leaves, and it's as if she takes some of the air in the room with her.

The absence of a third party makes this all way too surreal. A mini female Vadim is prancing around haughtily while the original, older Vadim stands rigid in the corner, watching her.

And then there's me, ogling them both with an increasing sense of panic. More than ever, I'm starting to sense what I was afraid of all along, that niggling suspicion that I don't belong here. I don't deserve to belong here.

Navigating awkward social situations in the past has taught me that the only way to banish such an emotion is to force some small talk and hope for the best.

"I… Um, why don't we show you to your room?" I croak, to break the silence.

Magda cocks her head at me, her gaze skeptical. "My *own* room?" she prods in that eerily charming yet cold cadence. "I don't have to share it?"

"No." I force out a strangled laugh. "Who would you share it with, sweetie?"

She eyes me directly and blinks once. "You. Aren't you the other guest in the house?"

I grit my teeth in shock. My gaze cuts to Vadim, who hasn't budged from his spot. He shakes his head, raking his hands through his hair.

"No," he croaks. "She's not—"

"Let's show you around," I say, jutting my chin with what I hope passes for poise. I start for the stairs. Within seconds, Vadim is by my side and, in our wake, resonate tiny, hesitant footsteps that trail behind during the entire ascent upstairs.

When we reach her room, Magda toes the threshold, eyeing everything with barely any expression. "It's okay, I guess," she declares after a few weighty seconds of silence. "I just wish…"

"What?" Vadim steps forward, suddenly animated, his jaw clenched. It's as if the prospect of disappointing her does something to him internally. Shatters him.

Magda sighs and tosses It onto the bed, unconcerned as his floppy head rebounds off the headboard. "I just wish it was yellow," she says, folding her arms over her black pinafore. "I hate blue."

"You do?" Vadim's expression further constricts. "But, Ms. Anderson—"

"She must have lied." Dismissively, she shrugs her shoulders and moves to stand before her window. Her fingers ruthlessly clutch at her forearms, but I don't miss how they twitch. Like someone aching to jump onto the window seat and peer through the glass in awe of the view. Or run their fingers through the fully stocked bookshelf. The more I watch her, the more I'm convinced. She's Vadim's through and through.

Meaning that every word and action is calculated and intentional. And right now, for whatever reason, she *wants* to see his guilt-ridden expression reflected off the window glass. In response to the sight, her small chin lowers, and her fingers grip her arms tighter in triumph.

"We'll let you get settled in," I suggest, reaching for Vadim's hand. His is shaking though his expression reveals nothing but cold, careful blankness.

"What would you like for dinner?" he asks, his tone level. "You can ask for anything. You may have it—"

"I'm not hungry." Whirling on her heel, Magda marches over and snatches her suitcase right from his grasp. She starts to place it down beside the bed only to notice something that makes her eyes widen as she pauses mid-act. "I have my own bathroom?"

My ears perk up. For a second, that haughty chirp cracked, revealing a hint of true excitement. As if aware of her failing façade, she kicks the suitcase over and sighs with the utmost nonchalance.

"Yes," Vadim says, though I don't think he noticed. He's too busy watching her. Gaping at her. If I'm stunned by the similarities in them both, I can't imagine what he must be feeling. "All of this is yours. Everything. And we can have the color changed tomorrow—"

"I'm tired." Magda crosses over to the door and grasps the handle. "Can I take a nap?"

Vadim blinks. "Of course."

"Okay." She proceeds to close the door, forcing us to scramble out into the hall. The resulting slam resonates through the walls.

I look at Vadim. His expression is more controlled than ever, crafted to avoid displaying a hint of real emotion. But he can't hide from me—not anymore. Confusion haunts his eyes as they meet mine, alluding to a pain he desperately scrambles to hide.

"Let's go see about lunch," he says.

I follow him into the kitchen, where I'm surprised to find the fridge and cupboards magically stocked with food fit for a child and not just enough sustenance to keep a reclusive billionaire alive. Ena's even made a series of new meals to fill the freezer, it seems. Color coded, to boot—blue lids contain the usual meat and vegetable entre that Vadim appears to prefer. Yellow, on the other hand, looks to be an array of child-friendly fare from chicken nuggets and fries to vegetables cut in all sorts of appealing shapes.

"I have got to get myself a henchman," I say as I examine another carefully crafted meal.

Vadim eyes me with the hint of a smile threatening his serious frown. "I have a feeling you'd be a lot more demanding than I am. Ena would love you as an employer."

"Maybe I'll rethink keeping my distance from him," I propose. "That is, if he can forgive me for forgetting to feed you before your standoff with your brother."

Vadim's grin falls flat, and a sudden thought makes me reach for his hand, stroking the back of it.

"Does he know?" I ask. "Maxim. About…"

"No," Vadim says, his teeth bared, eyes cold. "And as far as I'm concerned, he doesn't need to."

"He is her uncle," I say, but I'm not sure if I mean it as a question or a statement. I know firsthand that relationships, no matter how close, can dissipate overnight. Titles mean nothing. You can go from someone's wife one second, to a stranger the next—and vice versa apparently.

In search of a distraction, I turn my attention back to the freezer and rummage through the prepackaged meals. "I think I want chicken," I declare, deciding for us both.

Dutifully, Vadim places the platter in the oven while I stand on tiptoe to rummage through the cupboards above his head.

"I also think this occasion calls for a little daytime wine. Yes?"

He shoots me an amused look that makes my breath catch.

"I think I should buy shares in this company," he says while reading the label of my cherished vintage. "You must singlehandedly keep them afloat."

I simper. "What can I say? It's in my blood—" I break off as I spot a small figure watching us from the doorway, her arms crossed.

"There is a pool," she says carefully. Her tiny frown and stern gaze take on a harder edge, as if she's fighting to seem as disinterested as possible.

"Oh, that's right," I say, recalling the list Vadim and I had poured over. "You like to swim. Right?"

Magda says nothing, turning her attention to Vadim, who cautiously meets her gaze. It's like something unspoken passes between them, and they both promptly turn away, their jaws clenched.

"Never mind," Magda says, shrugging. "It's too cold to swim, anyway—"

"It's heated," Vadim says. He skirts the counter and advances toward her. "You can swim whenever you'd like. As long as I, Tiffany, or another adult is present."

Magda's lips twitch, but she forces a curt nod. "Okay."

"And there are acres of property," Vadim adds, ushering her into the foyer. I follow them at a distance, but close enough to hear him add, "We're having a playground built there—" he points to a section of budding construction visible through the row of windows in the living room. "And there is a boathouse if you're interested in going onto the water. And a stable…"

I'm so distracted watching them. I barely notice the muffled thud of advancing footsteps until the front door trembles beneath a thudding blow. Another. Then, as we all watch, the door flies open to reveal a hulking creature resonating so much rage he almost seems inhuman.

Maxim. His dark eyes fly to Vadim as he forms his hands into fists, and boldly crosses the threshold.

"Is this a game to you?" he demands, his accent so thick I can barely understand him. "Buying this house. Flaunting your ownership. To taunt me? I should—"

He plows into the foyer without seeming to notice the small figure nearly trampled in his path. Magda's eyes go bug-wide as her mouth contorts into a startled o-shape. I don't even think she manages to scream before she turns on her heel and runs.

But her target is already halfway to her. Without hesitation, Vadim snatches her into his arms, crushing her to his chest.

"Get out," he growls, holding his daughter protectively close. I've never seen him like this—eyes flashing, expression lethal. "Now."

Maxim falters, his body deflating as shock disrupts his furious features. He blinks, looking from Vadim, to Magda, and then me.

"You sick son of a bitch," he says incredulously. "You think this is a family? Where did you find her, huh?" He jerks his chin at Magda. "Off the fucking street? Did you kidnap her too—" He breaks off, and I have a sinking suspicion why. Magda, from the safety of Vadim's arms, glanced at him fearfully, turning far enough that he could see her face. A near mirror image of *Vadim's* face.

I can't describe the expression that befalls him next. As if struck, he staggers back a step, his massive body swaying before he manages to right himself, his gaze puzzled.

"Get out," Vadim snarls. "Now, so help me God. Don't make me resort to other methods. *Leave.*"

Maxim's nostrils flare as his lips open and close wordlessly. Then, without so much as a parting threat, he turns and barrels through the remains of the door.

"Ena," Vadim calls the second his brother disappears from view.

The stout bodyguard enters the foyer as if conjured from thin air, his expression gruff. "*Now* I secure perimeter?" he asks in his halting drawl. Simmering anger laces his tone, and I suspect I'm witnessing the tail end of an argument. Something to do with the property and securing it. Maxim had been able to waltz right through the front door—because Vadim had intentionally kept his security at bay?

Whatever his reasons for doing so, I assume they've quickly changed. "Yes," he says with a nod. "No one comes close without you handling them personally."

Ena nods and puffs up, satisfied. He crosses over to the remains of the door and inspects the damage. The confidence with which he does so makes me suspect that intervening after a violent situation isn't exactly an unusual occurrence for him.

Vadim steps back, moving toward the kitchen. His voice reaches me, a soothing, persistent hum that chokes my heart.

"*Chut, ma douce fille,*" he murmurs, stroking Magda's dark hair. "*Tout va bien. Tu es en sécurité…*"

He rocks her against him with such a gentle motion that I doubt he's even aware of it. She clings to him, her face in his chest, her tiny hands gripping him so tightly her knuckles are white.

He continues to speak to her in French until she finally draws back and wiggles free of his grasp. Her face is beet red, I notice as she turns and marches past me, storming up the stairs. A second later, presumably, her bedroom door slams shut, the thud resonating throughout the house.

"I'll kill him," Vadim says, but his tone is far too serious. He means it.

Thinking quickly, I approach him and lace my fingers through his hair, planting my lips against his collar. "No, you won't." I smooth my hands down his front and finger the very end of his tie. "You're going to help me make lunch for Magda. Then you're going to have Ena secure the property, hmm? And later, you will think of a *humane* way to confront your brother."

He stiffens. Cautiously, I feel his fingers sink through my hair as his arm encircles my waist, holding me close.

"*Oui*—yes," he says, his accent thick. I file away another quirk of his for later reflection—he switches to French when overwhelmed, or protective, which gives a greater semblance to the words he murmured to me the other night. *Tell me you'll stay with me. That I can give you what you need, oui?*

Overwhelmed, I draw back and turn my attention to the freezer. "Nuggets, or broccoli and cheese shaped like dinosaurs? Which do you think she'd like?"

He makes a low sound in his throat as he inspects his options. "I never was a fan of food crafted to look like other forms of food," he says skeptically.

"Nuggets, it is!" I hand him the container to heat up while I head for the stairs, skirting Ena, who found a set of tools from somewhere and is working on the door with vigor.

My heart skips as I approach Magda's room though I'm not sure why. Perhaps because I'm breaking another one of my impromptu rules—stay out of this. Let Vadim get to know his daughter in peace, no matter how awkward a process it might turn out to be.

So much for that.

"Magda?" I gather the nerve to knock on her door and gingerly push it open.

A sweet, soft melody drifts out. Halting. A song? The foreign words are uttered with meticulous care. French? It has to be. Every syllable is pronounced in an accent fitting enough to match Vadim's—but overly careful as if parroted rather than fluent mastery of the language. Lost in concentration, she's standing on the window seat, her hands braced against the window while her bear sits propped against her feet. She sings mindlessly while scanning the horizon with such an inquisitive expression I stop short.

She goes rigid and whips around to face me, her eyes narrowing. The song dies mid-phrase, and she crosses her arms once more.

"Can I help you?" she asks, her tone shrill but polite.

"Are you settling in okay?" I warily step inside the room. Her suitcase is open, various items strewn across the bed. A few pieces of clothing, a worn looking leather-bound book, and another stuffed animal, though one lacking the signs of surgery that It sports. Beside the lot is a small pink carrying case that looks as though it's seen better days.

The moment my eyes settle on it, Magda jumps from the window seat and crosses to the bed. Meeting my gaze, she deliberately grabs her belongings and shoves them back into the suitcase, slamming it shut.

"I'm fine," she says. "Thanks."

"Okay." I force a smile and turn for the door. "We'll be just downstairs, and we made lunch—"

"I'm not a baby, you know." Gone is the façade of politeness. Her tone is so cutting that I can only think of one comparison fitting enough to match the icy hostility—the insistence of a certain billionaire that I wasn't his type, for instance.

I turn to face her, sensing my eyebrow raise. "I didn't mean to imply that you were."

"Who are you anyway?" She appraises me with a haughty flick of her chin, her arms crossed. "You're not married to him. Even if you do have a ring on." She nods to my left hand, and I clench said fingers into a fist, caught.

My cheeks flame, but something prevents me from backing down. Instead, I advance a step toward her, keeping my tone level. "And if I'm not?"

She bites her lower lip and seems to mull it over. Then she smiles, and it's such a beautiful match to Vadim's. The one he wears when his aim is cruel. "Did you read my file?" she asks sweetly, batting her eyelashes. "My last family, the Robinsons, are moving to the other side of the country, just to get away from me." Her smile grows wider as if she's utterly pleased with that fact.

But her eyes are every bit as expressive as her father's, revealing the truth in snippets that require deciphering.

"I don't know what I did to scare them so much," she says, throwing her hands into the air. "Maybe it was when I tried to microwave the cat?"

Any other time, with any other child, I'd be rightfully disgusted. Fearful, even. Maybe I should be in this case? I don't know what it is about her gleeful, ghoulish expression that makes me perch on the end of her bed and cross my legs casually.

"Is that all?" I ask, an eyebrow raised. "I once threatened to turn my father's prized stallion into glue. I even looked up the number for what I thought was the glue factory. Then I ran away with a duffle filled with barbie dolls and an entire box of pop tarts."

She blinks, caught off guard.

"I didn't make it far, mind you." I extend my fingers, inspecting the pink polish. "I was barely past the tennis courts before I chickened out. Besides, I didn't really want to hurt old Dauntless, anyway. I just wanted to make my parents squirm." It's an odd story to relay so bluntly. Something I predictably wouldn't tell most people on our first meeting.

Magda frowns, unsure of how to process it.

"Did the Robinsons do something to you that made you want to make them squirm?" I ask, free of judgment.

She purses her lips. "No. But what if I want to make *you* squirm?"

"Hmm." I think it over, then I lean forward and meet her gaze head-on. If I'm not mistaken, she flinches and takes a small step back. "Then try harder. I may look like a dumb bimbo, but I too, went through a hellion phase. Whatever you're thinking, whatever you're planning—trust me, baby, I wrote the book."

She wrinkles her nose, seemingly more confused than ever. "Why?" she demands.

I shrug as if the answer is obvious. "I wanted attention. I wanted to make my dad feel guilty. I wanted my mom to stop day drinking and look at me. I was bored. What made you want to provoke the Robinsons?"

Her piercing eyes narrow further. "You're weird," she declares, returning to her suitcase. She wrenches it open, and one by one withdraws what seems to be her few personal belongings. Displaying another one of Vadim's quirks, she meticulously folds a cream-colored sweater and reaches for an orange shirt.

"We can take you shopping if you'd like," I say, volunteering the use of Vadim's magic credit card. "Do you like dresses? Pants?"

She doesn't answer, preferring to sort her few outfits, leaving her book and stuffed animal on the bed. The case she grabs last. "This has to go in the fridge," she says with all of the maturity of a miniature adult, not a seven-year-old. "It's my insulin."

"Okay. We'll throw it in when we go downstairs. How about we speed things along?" I reach for a neatly folded jacket. "I can help you put these away—"

"Why?" Her tone isn't quite as hostile, but her dark brows are furrowing, her frown skeptical. God, it's so much like interacting with Vadim. Someone constantly on guard, mistrustful of any hint of kindness. For a horrible second, I wonder if his daughter's upbringing was even a fraction as horrific as his. Then I push the thought away and tug the jacket from her grip, moving toward her closet as she watches on in shock.

"You have beautiful hair," I tell her, ignoring the question. "I can braid it for you tonight, if you want. I used to love when my mom did that."

"But you aren't my mom," she snipes almost in a singsong tone.

I ignore the bait and snatch an empty hanger from one of the many rails lining her very own massive walk-in closet. My brain skips ahead, envisioning all of the various clothing items she'll need to stock it with. Pajamas. Day clothing. Night clothing. Dress-up clothing. If dressing her father was a challenge, I assume she'll be just as surly to shop for. A challenge I'm willing to accept.

"Here," I tell her, holding out my hand for the sweater in her grip. "Let me put your things away. Then we'll go get some lunch, huh?"

So surly. So wary. To my surprise, she reluctantly steps forward and relinquishes the sweater. As I hang it, she reappears with the rest of her clothing balanced in her arms.

"What's your name?" she asks almost grudgingly as I arrange her clothing according to color.

"Tiffany."

She accepts the introduction with a sniff. "I'm hungry."

I hang her last shirt and switch off the light. "I think the food should be ready. Let's go check."

She follows as I descend the stairs and enter the kitchen to find Vadim at the counter, dividing the contents of the platters between three plates. While I stow Magda's pink insulin case into the fridge, he looks up, his expression almost panicked. *Help me,* I imagine him begging were he desperate enough to do so out loud. *Don't leave me.*

I smile to reassure him.

"I hope you like nuggets," I tell Magda as I take a seat at the table.

She claims the one across from me but frowns as Vadim places a plate down in front of her. Warily, she nudges a nugget with the tip of her finger before taking a hesitant bite. Ena's cooking must win her over because all reluctance drains from her face, and she doesn't need any more prompting.

I watch her, so distracted by the sight of her that I barely notice as Vadim sits beside me. Pretty soon, we're *both* staring at her, his beautiful little girl, unaware of the nearness of her biological father. Or how much he loves her already. His fingers twitch as she reaches for a glass of water as if he has to stop himself from grabbing it for her. When she finishes her food, he's already racing across the kitchen in search of a napkin.

"Am I still going to my school?" Magda asks, pushing her plate aside.

"Yes." Vadim offers her a napkin that she doesn't take. Awkwardly he sets it beside her and circles the table to reclaim his seat. "After the break. Don't worry about any disruptions."

"Okay," she says, eyeing her tiny fingers. "And I can have new clothes?"

"Anything," Vadim rasps.

Magda fixates her steely gaze on me. "And *you'll* take me?"

"If you want," I say cautiously. "We could go tomorrow?"

She shrugs and sips from her water. "Okay."

I don't think I'm the only one who misses the fact that Vadim is pointedly left out of her invitation.

"Can I go up to my room now?"

"Y-Yes—" Vadim barely gets the word out before she's skipping merrily across the kitchen. Her tiny steps echo as she marches up the stairs, and once again, her door slams with force.

Vadim sighs, his jaw clenched, his gaze on the table. One of his hands forms a fist over the glass surface, the knuckles whitening.

I gingerly cradle his fingers with my own and lean down, kissing the rigid peaks. Then I feather another kiss over his wrist, up to his collar. Higher, until I finally reach his lips.

"You did good," I insist as his mouth remains stubbornly closed. "You did so good—"

"Have I?" He withdraws from me and stands, tearing at his hair with both hands. "I need to work," he says. "I'll be in the study."

I watch him go, more conflicted than ever. Can I withstand two switchblade humans battling their emotions? My heart throbs in a way that gives me serious doubt.

CHAPTER NINE

Left to my own devices, I pour myself a fresh glass of wine and decide to take my chances exploring the outside of the house. A small glass door near the back of the kitchen leads onto a stone terrace surrounding the private pool. Beyond, stretches the waterfront lined by a rocky beach that conjures the potential for plenty of warm, fuzzy memories to be made. The more I take in the view, the more I feel for my beautiful, tormented Vadim. The poor man had to have envisioned the same images I am.

Magda, playing in the pool or skipping happily by the water. Her, fishing water toys from the boathouse or racing off to the stable in the distance. Him, showing her how to ride his white mare, Zzazza...

As if summoned by the thought, I sense the door open behind me as a looming figure steps onto the terrace. "I come with an offering of contrition."

I turn to find Vadim exiting the kitchen, a wine glass in tow. Beaming, I gladly accept his token. "You are forgiven, peon," I tell him, taking a sip.

He settles against me from behind, his hands capturing my waist. It's such an intimate position—I should balk, I think. Maybe I'm too tired, lulled by the promise of wine? Or I'm lying to myself, desperate to escape the obvious. It feels so *natural* being with him like this, and my ever-present list feels further away.

"Thank you for staying," he says against my scalp.

Gratitude nearly knocks me over, and I hastily take a second sip of wine to steel myself. "Don't mention it."

Together, we watch the sun scuttle across the horizon, each of us envisioning a million potential uses for the beautiful property. Will any of them ever come to fruition? Who knows?

I, for one, am willing to hope for as much.

Eventually, I bring myself to brush my hand along his forearm. "We should get ready for dinner," I suggest, though a part of me wishes I could spend the night in his arms, just enjoying the vastness of his property.

As if to spoil the potential of that ever happening, we both turn as the sliding glass door is noisily wrenched open from the inside.

"I'm hungry," Magda declares, her tone flat. She scans the waiting pool and the waterfront beyond with feigned disinterest. But her eyes linger over the bay, in particular, a rare gleam of hunger coloring her irises. Just as quickly, it vanishes, snuffed out with a surly pout. "I'm really hungry."

"What would you like? Whatever you wish," Vadim says, moving toward her.

She crosses her arms, her lips pursed thoughtfully. "The Robinsons never let me have pizza," she says.

"Because of the carbohydrate content," Vadim explains, following her into the kitchen. "We need to be careful about how much we consume and always make sure to cover our meals with enough insulin."

"We?" She stares as he lifts his shirt, revealing the tubing of his pump. He uses it so rarely around me, I've almost forgotten the device's existence.

"*We*," he reiterates. "Luckily for us both, I know of a pizzeria that creates an amazing low carb pie. Name your toppings."

She thoughtfully taps her chin. "Cheese and pepperoni."

"Done." He pulls a cell phone from his pocket and steps aside to phone in the order while I back into a corner and watch them both. There is something so beautiful in seeing them interact together, each cautious in their own right.

When he's done on the phone, Vadim approaches the fridge and grabs a pitcher of orange juice. "Set the table?" he asks Magda.

She doesn't agree out loud, but she gradually moves to the cupboard he indicates and accepts the three plates he gives her.

I don't inch forward until the table is set, and Vadim is pouring three glasses of juice to place at each setting. "What else do you like in addition to pizza?" he asks her.

"Cake," she says, and I get the sense she's deliberately provoking him.

With an adept social grace, Vadim doesn't even seem to notice the bait. "I know of a bakery as well that makes a delicious cake. What else?"

She proceeds to play a devious game of naming foods that are not diabetic-friendly, while he patiently counters each one with a sugar-free alternative. It's as if he studied the list of foods a child may crave and ensured that he had a ready supply of options for her.

In fact, I'm sure that's the case.

Finally bored, Magda proceeds to tap her slender fingers along the table. Noticing the act, Vadim asks, "Do you play any instruments?"

She wrinkles her nose. "Maybe."

"I loved playing the piano when I was your age," he says softly. "When I could find one."

"The Robinsons didn't have a piano." She folds her arms, her chin jutting.

"I can get you one." He makes it sound as simple as snapping his fingers. "And lessons, if you'd like."

She mulls it over, and I half-expect her to refuse. I think a part of her wants to. But like him, she's too curious, drawn to an opportunity to tackle something new. While Vadim chooses to research BDSM, she'll warily accept his offer of musical training.

"Okay."

"I'll make the arrangements first thing in the morning."

We sit in awkward silence until the pizza arrives, courtesy of a gruff Ena who manages up what I think might be a smile once he spots Magda. We eat together, saying nothing until finally, Magda sets her plate aside.

"I'm tired," she says.

"Do you need someone to tuck you in?" Vadim starts to stand, but she shoots him a look so withering he falters.

"I'm not a baby," she says, her nose in the air. She flounces from the room and up the stairs. Predictably, the door slams.

"Give her time," I say, approaching Vadim from behind. I run my fingers over the muscles of his back, sliding around to his front. When I toy with the waistband of his pants, he sucks in a deep breath.

"Restraint is one skill we will both have to learn," he says hoarsely.

"I know." I nuzzle the back of his neck even as my fingers obediently withdraw. "Just know that I find you trying to be super dad incredibly sexy. I wish to do all sorts of naughty things to you when little ears are finally asleep."

"Oh?" He turns to face me, an eyebrow raised. I shiver as he draws me close, letting my body mold against his. "What kinds of things?"

"Well…" I stand on tiptoe and murmur a list of sordid, X-rated options into his ear. "And that's to start."

"You are insatiable." He runs his fingers down my back as his eyes lower to mine. "And patient. And… I couldn't do this without you."

A part of me despairs at the fact that he actually seems to mean it. "Yes, you could," I argue. It's the truth. "She's resistant to you, but that's because you're both so alike. In no time, you'll have her madly in love with you. Just like—" I manage to physically stop myself from saying more by slamming my hand over my mouth.

His eyes narrow, and he snatches the fingers in question, drawing them away. Something between us shifts from sizzling lust to a smoldering heat I feel deep in my core.

"Madly in love," he says as if tasting the words for the very first time. "Like?"

"Sir!"

We break apart as Ena storms into the kitchen, his expression sterner than ever. "Visitor," he says to Vadim. "Mr. Hood. I let him in?"

I look at Vadim in awe as he seems to physically bite back a groan. Finally, he nods. "Yes. Let him in."

Ena races off, and Vadim turns to me, cradling my cheek against his palm before I can pull away.

"Check on Magda for me?"

"Okay," I concede without prying as to who this mysterious visitor might be. I can't resist placing a soft kiss along his jaw —just one.

Upstairs, I find the door to Magda's room ajar. True to her insistence on the fact, she *isn't* a baby, more than capable of getting herself ready for bed. She's already dressed in a pair of pajamas, her damp curls hanging down her shoulders as she moves about her room, dragging It by his floppy, reattached head. When she spots me staring, she eyes me without comment, glancing me up and down with a flick of her unnerving eyes.

"Goodnight," I say, closing the door behind me as I reenter the hall.

"Wait."

I return to find her rummaging through an end table for an object that she marches toward me and offers up without a word. A worn, wooden hairbrush.

Like a princess used to dolling out commands, she sits on her bed with her back to me.

"Braids?" I suggest as I dutifully approach her and smooth my fingers through her thick ringlets. Gosh, her hair is every bit as beautiful as her father's. I brush through it all gently and arrange two plaits when she doesn't offer up a complaint either way.

As soon as I finish the final braid, she lurches to her feet and snatches the brush. Then she climbs under the blankets, tucking It under her arm.

"Goodnight," I murmur as I escape this time without a word from her.

A small smile shapes my mouth as I return downstairs. Before I remember that, I shouldn't be doing things like tucking my one-night-too-many-stand's daughter into bed. If anything, I should be putting distance between us.

And her father.

The man whose voice alone makes me quiver, even now as he speaks to someone else, his tone low and strained. "...I didn't know until two years ago. For obvious reasons, it's not something I'm eager to discuss."

"*That's* why you went off all that bloody time," a man replies, his accent distinctly British. "I thought it might have been because your old partner died, but... You didn't think to ask for fucking help?"

"I thought it was best to keep her separate from me," Vadim says. Even from this distance, I can picture his expression—tortured, guilty eyes, and a tight frown. My heart aches, and I long to run my fingers through his hair until his devious grin returns in full. "I've changed my mind since."

"Why?" the other man demands. I think I recognize his voice —*Milton.*

A low sound issues from Vadim that could be a laugh from a normal man. "Why not? If Maxim can become father of the year, I can't? My daughter is at least *mine.*"

"But how? Don't tell me you knocked-up some woman and just left her. That's not like you."

Vadim's silent for so long. Finally, he sighs. "Do you remember my last owner?" he asks, his tone gruff. "The one they called The Collector?"

"I remember him, the sick fuck," Milton snarls. I imagine his handsome visage twisted with anger, his dark eyes narrowed. "I remember the rumors as well. Don't tell me…"

"They're true." Vadim sounds so cold. So distant. A stranger. "He had that name for a reason. His *collection.* He always spoke of breeding his favorite toys, be them animals, or…"

I'm drawn forward three more steps before I have the sense to stop at the base of the staircase. Their voices must be coming from the study—I don't see anyone in the foyer or the living room.

"He must have stored his samples in a place where they were spared from the purge. I'd thought I'd burned everything else to the fucking ground."

"Samples?" Milton's tone conveys enough horror for us both. "Fuck! Do you know who her mother is? And how could his *samples*… Maxim said she's young. That bastard died over a decade ago."

"I don't know why or how she was born," Vadim admits. "As for her mother… I do have one hunch. You might even remember her."

"Another 'favorite?'" Milton asks, hissing the term.

"Her name was Irina." I've never heard Vadim's tone so detached. Broken. "Magda has her eyes. If I would consider anyone an ally in that world, other than you… But most would not understand our relationship," he adds. "With your convenient knowledge in psychiatry, I think you'd deem it something along the lines of… *Unhealthy codependency with anti-social attributes.*"

"Oh?"

"You know what it's like," Vadim says softly. "When you question your own humanity. When you crave validation and power so badly, you'll do anything to find it? Confide in *anyone.*"

"I understand," Milton says, his voice a rasp.

"Irina and I were more partners than anything else. In manipulation. Deception. Seduction. We made a game of it. Stealing tokens to prove who was the better player. Looking back, I think it was the only way we could survive. She disappeared before I gained my freedom," he adds. "Whether she was killed or escaped, I never found out. But now I suspect she left on her own. Left me behind. To her, it would be just another part of the game."

"And your child?" Milton presses. "Is she part of the 'game'? Have you tried to find her, Irina? You cite my 'psychiatric' experience, which you gladly make use of. And yet, in all of our sessions, you've never mentioned her."

"I don't know," Vadim says in a tone that makes something inside me throb. "If she is alive...she's deliberately concealed herself from me. When I found Magda, she had no documentation. No birth certificate. It's like she appeared out of nowhere, but the doctor who did her first examination claimed that she had been well-fed beforehand. Well-groomed and her vaccinations appeared to be up to date. The only abnormality was that her diabetes was dangerously uncontrolled."

"Could she have been planted?" Milton wonders. "Where you would find her."

"If Irina is her mother..." He trails off in that way he does when he's mulling something over. Something puzzling like the prospect of me leaving, or a woman who may or may not be the mother of his child. "Why have I never mentioned her? We all had our ways of coping," he adds softly. "She could see those around her as creatures to protect or toys just as easily. When she left, there was no point in dwelling on her. She would *want* me to dwell. And now? I don't see her abandoning Magda without a reason."

"A fucked up one from what it sounds like," Milton hisses. "I have to ask. Was... Was she part of the trade, your girl?"

"No," Vadim says, and I sense them both release sighs of relief. "Her examinations revealed no sign of abuse. She's had a relatively normal upbringing. No matter her origin, I will protect her."

"And you won't be alone in that." The heat in Milton's tone challenges Vadim's own assurance. *"Milton sees me as a scared little boy he's sworn to protect.*" But duty is a very different animal from unquestionable loyalty. "Can I see her?" he asks.

"She's sleeping," Vadim says. "Maybe tomorrow. But she doesn't know who I am for now. As far as she's concerned, I'm her new foster placement."

"Damn." Milton whistles. "Do you plan on telling her?"

"Maybe. When the time is right."

"And here I thought Maxim could be a secretive prick. He hides his women from me. You hide your children. What a friendship we all share."

"You know I trust you more than anyone," Vadim says, sounding closer. Advancing footsteps force me to scamper up the stairs just as the two men appear in the foyer, advancing toward the front door.

"And you deserve to meet her," Vadim adds.

"And Maxim?" Milton draws up beside him, fingering the collar of his crisp, ebony suit. "I hear he didn't make the best impression."

"*He* won't be coming anywhere near her," Vadim says coldly. "I tried with him. But he's proven more than once—he isn't worth the time. As far as Magda is concerned, he's a violent stranger who barged into her home and scared the hell out of her."

Milton frowns. "For what it's worth, he didn't mean to scare her."

"The fact that he's saying as much through you and not in person is all I need to know." Vadim's gaze darkens, closed-off. "He will never see her again."

Milton shrugs as Vadim opens the front door. "I hope you change your mind," he says before stepping out into the darkness. "That little girl needs all of the family she can get. You know better than anyone else that one can't be too picky when it comes to that subject."

He leaves, and Vadim closes the door after him, sighing. Rather than escape before he catches me eavesdropping, I take a moment to ogle him. His shoulders are rigid, his profile the picture of brooding unease. As I watch, his constricted expression softens as his lips part, his voice rasping, "My beauty," he calls to me despite my hiding place. "So cunning. So sly. How much did you hear?"

I step around the corner and descend the stairs, my chin jutting in defiance. "Enough to know I deserve to be punished." I force a smile, praying that I seem nonchalant enough to have missed the trigger points of his conversation. Like the mysterious Irina who shares Magda's electric-blue eyes. Naughty questions persist on the fringes of my brain anyway. Such as, *did he love her? Is he hoping she'll return?*

I could ask him.

I should…

But I can't.

His gaze is far too guarded, and I don't have the heart to shatter my ruse. I saunter to him instead and grab his tie, stroking the fabric suggestively.

"Should I be spanked for my insolence?" I wonder, making my voice low enough so that it won't carry upstairs. "Or do I deserve a harsher chastisement?"

Vadim cinches my waist in both hands, yanking me closer. I finger his collar while his mouth finds my ear, nibbling at the lobe. "You deserve the world," he growls in a tone that makes my head spin. So insistent. So confident in that regard.

A world of his making. A sinful, kinky paradise in which I'm at his mercy—helpless as he pulls me down the hall and into his study, taking care not to make too much noise. I smother a moan as he strips me, leaving the façade of his perfect fake wife on the floor before he spreads me over his desk and doles out my punishment.

I nearly scream as he latches his mouth above my piercing, thrusting with his tongue until I'm incoherent. This is true torture—having to stay silent amid the tumult of pleasure he gives me. Ruthlessly, he gives it. Over and over until I'm wracked with sobs as tears stream down my face in my quest to smother all noise.

I praise him with drawn nails raking through his hair instead. With orgasms that leave him groaning in their wake. Limp and panting, all I can do is lie helplessly as he stands and frees his cock from the confines of his slacks.

I take him deep on the first thrust, hissing in pleasure, my eyelids fluttering. I don't know if it's the location, or the tension that comes from sneaking around but I come damn near instantly, and he isn't far behind, snatching me to him as he spills inside me.

We come back to clinging to any part of each other we can reach. As my breathing returns to normal, I find his ear, my voice a whisper.

"I feel sufficiently punished," I tell him.

He chuckles and draws back to stare down on me with those haunting, brooding eyes. "Enough to repent?" he wonders, stroking the hair from my face. "For ever wanting to leave me?"

I nod even as a part of me warns me to back down. Avoid. Salvage our one fragile boundary. "I believe your torturous methods are making progress with this prisoner," I confess despite myself. "For better or for worse."

"Better," he insists, drawing me into his arms while scanning the floor for our scattered clothing. "This is better."

And he sounds so damn confident.

I almost believe him.

CHAPTER TEN

I blink my eyes open, unsure of what drew me awake in the first place. I'm on the bed, I think, judging from the softness beneath me. Weak sunlight pours in through the window, illuminating the empty space beside me—Vadim is gone.

Sighing, I slump against a pillow, stroking the silken sheets he'd laid on beside me. Kinky sex is a drug unto itself, but I don't think anything tops being held by him. Falling asleep to the sound of his heartbeat while his breaths ruffle my hair. This man will be the end of me, in a way Jim could only dream.

Fuck the list. With every passing second, I'm growing resigned to my fate—but that doesn't mean I can't enjoy every fucking minute.

I halfheartedly scan the rest of the room though I sense without having to check that he isn't here. Sure enough, the doorway to the bathroom is empty, as is the rest of the room…

Or not. I bolt upright, clutching the sheet to my front as my eyes blink to bring the tiny figure watching me from the foot of the bed into focus.

"M-Magda?" I croak.

She's fully dressed, her dark hair neatly brushed back behind a scarlet headband. Another black pinafore over a white shirt makes her look like some tiny, less demonic version of Wednesday Adams. At least until I spot the once decapitated bear dangling from her arm.

"Are we going shopping today?" she asks, unconcerned as I scramble to make sure I'm fully covered and that any silver toys are hidden from view.

"Um… Where is your fath—Mr. Vadim?" I ask.

She shrugs. "I don't know. It's six a.m.," she adds. "I've been up since five."

And Vadim's been gone since then? Frowning, I try to pinpoint any time during the night when he could have left, but I can't remember. Facing Magda, I'm left with no choice.

"Well, um, why don't you go into the closet and find me something to wear, huh? My stuff is on the left-hand side."

She frowns but obediently scuttles off, and I take the brief freedom from tiny eyes to race into the bathroom and jump into the shower. I wash off quickly and thank God that Vadim had the sense to stash a few robes here, hanging on a hook near the shower entrance. I select a black one that smells like him and shimmy into it. When I return to the bedroom, I find Magda sitting patiently on a leather chair by the window, nearly swallowed by a sea of hot pink faux fur perched on her lap.

"You actually wear this?" she asks, lifting what appears to be the sleeve of my favorite jacket between two fingers.

"Yeah." I gently take the jacket from her grasp, discovering a purple, frothy dress underneath. Frowning, I eye them both, impressed by the potential. "Interesting color choice, Ms. Magda."

Her expression doesn't reveal either way if she picked the clothing on purpose or as a joke. When I pop into the bathroom to change, I'm stunned to find a flattering ensemble. Bold. Daring. Fluffy. The perfect outfit to tackle the challenge this day is shaping up to throw my way.

Magda, however, doesn't seem very impressed. She crushes It to her chest while sweeping her gaze over me with abject disinterest. "I'm hungry."

"Okay…" I exhale nervously. *Don't panic, Tiffy.* If I'm lucky, Ena packed away some breakfast in one of his prepared meals. "Come on. I'll make you something to eat."

Downstairs, I quickly discover no luck in terms of the prepackaged breakfast department. Luckily, Ena seemed to have countered such a lack by stocking the pantry with more— relatively healthy and carb controlled—colorful cereal than I think I've ever seen stocked in a grocery store at one time. After Magda picks out her preference, I make her a bowl and watch her eat while chewing on a croissant. She has a pump I quickly discover as she slips it from the pocket of her pinafore and programs her dosage of insulin.

"You need any help?" I ask.

The humorless look she directs my way is all the answer I need.

Within a few minutes, it's painfully clear that Vadim isn't down here either. Neither is he in the study when I gather the nerve to creep down the hall and check. Again, I wrack my brain, trying to remember anything from last night that might give me a clue as to his whereabouts.

I remember…

Warmth. I can recall the sensation of soft lips nudging my throat in reverence and a husky voice murmuring praises, even while half asleep. *"…beautiful. So beautiful. Mine."*

And then I remember a sudden chill as he pulled away. A noise in the distance. A phone call? He'd left the bed to take it, I think, speaking in a hushed tone.

How did I forget this before? My lust-drugged brain is sluggish with the details, and I rub at my temples until bit by bit more snippets return. He'd sounded…worried, I think. His tone had been gruffer than usual, deepening by the second. I think he'd been frantic afterward, moving through the dark, throwing on clothing.

How in the hell had I missed that?

"Did you hear me?" I blink and refocus on the source of the soft, irritated voice. Magda watches me frowning with her hands neatly folded beside her now-empty cereal bowl. "*Now* are we going shopping?"

"I…" I glance around, unsure of where Vadim even keeps his car keys, let alone any necessary numbers or emergency information in case we need them. "We should probably wait for your fath— Mr. Vadim to come back—"

"Mr. Vadim no come back." The stern grunt comes from Ena, who appears at the mouth of the kitchen, his arms crossed over the front of his battered leather jacket. "He busy. I take."

"You'll take us shopping?" Magda stands and smooths her hands down the front of her crisp pinafore. Taking It by his mangled head, she warily approaches Ena. As haughty as a little queen's, her voice reaches back to me, "Can we go now?"

"I guess…" Though I'm tempted to prod Ena for more details. Maybe I would if he didn't deliberately seem to avoid eye contact with me. As I approach him, he sticks out his hand, grudgingly offering me a single, small object.

"Mr. Vadim said to give you this."

This being his fancy, smanshy credit card. Only when I scan the name printed on the front, I nearly faint. It's mine. Or a version of mine, at least: *Tiffany Gorgoshev.*

"We go now," Ena says, snapping me from my shock. He waddles to the front door with Magda prancing in tow.

And I wonder if I'm already in far too deep.

ONCE WE REACH the downtown shopping district, I fight to push all concerns for Vadim out of my head. It's surprisingly easy once I enter the first boutique, and it becomes readily apparent that, for all of her reserved surliness, Ms. Magda may harbor a secret love for fashion.

More than once, I catch her gazing longingly at the smaller versions of the adult designs adorning various mannequins. After our personal saleswoman shows us to a private dressing room, I decide to put my suspicions to the test.

"Well?" I sit casually on a leather chaise and sip from a glass of customary wine—I'd argue with Vadim about the credit card later, but being married to a billionaire at least on paper certainly has its perks. "Show me your favorite outfits?" I dare her.

And for once, Magda squirms, her lips pursed with unease. I catch her gaze dart to an outfit near the back of the boutique that draws even my interest—a turquoise sweater dress with a bold, black collar and a matching headband.

Shopping for a little girl is a different animal from what I'm used to. Everything is too damn adorable, screaming to adorn tiny limbs. My brain skips ahead, picturing her any one of several designer fashions, complete with a cute hairstyle to match.

Reign it in, Tiffy, I scold myself.

"What kinds of clothing do you like?" I ask, desperate for a distraction.

She shrugs, crossing her arms. "The Robinsons never took me shopping," she says, her nose wrinkling. "I just got the old clothes."

I picture the smug Mrs. Robinson with a renewed rage.

"Well, we have the time." God only knows where Vadim's gone. "Let's see what you've got in terms of style, kid."

When the saleswoman returns to our corner, however, I take the lead and point her to the turquoise outfit, much to Magda's shock. "We'll try that one first."

Magda stares on in silence as the woman brings her the garments in the correct size. Her frown remains stubbornly in place as she creeps into a dressing room. But as she reappears minutes later, I clap my hands, pleased.

"You look beautiful! Turn around." Much like her father, blue is so her color. The hue enhances her eyes and alights the small, fleeting smile that shapes her mouth before she realizes it and frowns in earnest.

"It's…decent," she says crisply. "Just okay."

"*Okay*," I parrot with a knowing wink. "We'll take that one," I tell the saleswoman without bothering to hear the price.

"Now, what about that one?" I point to a red ensemble hanging across the showroom with an adult set to match. "We can both try it."

Magda says nothing, but when the saleswoman returns with the chosen clothing, she enters the dressing room beside the one I claim.

And I start to hope that this may not end in flames.

IT ISN'T until well after nightfall that we return to the house. By the time Ena and I approach the backseat and fish through the mound of shopping bags gathered there, Magda is fast asleep. She's small enough that I can easily carry her inside while Ena extends our tense truce by gathering up our combined purchases.

She's so beautiful, I'm mesmerized with every step it takes to enter the house. She has Vadim's long eyelashes that ghost her delicate cheekbones. Her glossy hair is freshly blown out into soft waves—courtesy of a trip to the salon after shopping—and her newly painted nails cling to It even in sleep. Something tightens in my chest the more I watch her while gingerly stepping over the threshold.

A day spent with a seven-year-old should sound horrifying in theory—had it been with most of my Sunday school class it would have been. But she's such a strange, unusual creature. I'm afraid I may be as intrigued by her as I am by the figure pacing anxiously in the foyer, his expression constricted.

"Thank God," he says, advancing toward me. "You're back."

I can't get a read on his expression as he leans in to press his lips to mine. Then he turns his attention to Magda and cradles her head gently while lifting her from my arms.

They make a breathtaking picture together. Him, in a dark navy suit, his hair slightly mussed as if he'd spent most of the day raking his fingers through it. Bundled in his arms, she looks like a doll wearing an ebony faux fur jacket and one of her new dresses—a gray slip with white applique flowers decorating the hem.

"You can kiss your billions goodbye in about ten years," I inform him softly. "I'm afraid to inform you that your daughter has all the signs of a budding shopaholic. Trained by yours truly, she's going to spend you out of house and home if you aren't careful."

His upper lip quirks into a pained smile as he smooths the wayward curls from Magda's face. "I'll just have to work harder then," he murmurs. "If I am to support *both* of your habits."

Both. I don't argue with that as he heads upstairs, entering Magda's room. He sets her gingerly on the bed while I scour her closet for a worn pair of pajamas. Something she said earlier makes my heart ache, and her few meager belongings take on a new significance. I don't say anything to Vadim though as we gently undress her and ease her into a nightdress. He tucks her beneath the blankets afterward, smoothing them over her with heartbreaking care. After ensuring that It is tucked in as well, we escape her room and instinctively head downstairs, putting as much distance between her and us. It's only when we're in the kitchen that I feel safe to talk again.

"She told me her foster family only gave her hand-me-downs," I say as we settle in at the island counter.

Vadim frowns, stroking his jaw. "That can't be right... I gave them access to an account specifically for her—with more than enough funds. Under the guise of a donation, of course. They've been making regular withdrawals."

"Well, they haven't been spoiling her, at least," I say halfheartedly. Inside, I'm more than happy to permanently vilify the Robinsons. Good riddance. "She was like a kid in a candy store today. Where were you?" I try to phrase the question as innocently as I can—but his reaction catches me off guard. He stiffens, his gaze distant.

"You took care of her," he says thickly. "Thank you."

I shiver as he reaches out, brushing my cheek in a gentle caress. His nearness is almost enough to make me bite back more questions. Something is bothering him. I can sense it in his eyes and what he doesn't say. His hands shake, and his paleness betrays that he hasn't eaten recently, if at all today.

"Let me make you some dinner," I say, turning to the freezer in search of one of Ena's meals. "Magda and I already ate. I made sure to check her sugars, and I took her to a restaurant with low carb options."

Though the latter part is entirely due to Ena, who seemed to know a list of suitable options by heart.

Vadim watches me as I select a chicken and veggie dish and heat it up for him. Minutes later, we trade places as I watch him dig in.

"She's a weird little girl, your kid," I tell him wryly. "She loves fashion, though I think she didn't want me to notice. She loves turquoise, especially. And black. I hope you don't mind, but we got our nails done, and that's the color she picked—"

"Thank you." He looks at me with such an expression. It steals my breath away and makes my skin catch fire in a strange, inexplicable way. Like I'm burning alive from the inside out, but it's a fire I wouldn't extinguish for the whole world.

"You say that like it was hard," I counter. "Being around her. Being around you."

Mayday, Tiffy, a part of me warns.

But his façade slips again. Whatever kept him away today is still haunting him. Distracting him. He looks so…tormented. The same, closed-off man I met in a hotel bar with his invisible wall firmly up.

When he clears his plate, we wash the dishes and eventually migrate into his study, where he claims the chair behind his desk. The second the door closes behind us, I sidle to him before I can stop myself and climb directly onto his lap, toying with the end of his tie. He sucks in a breath, his gaze cutting up to mine. Those dark eyes of his are endless—soul-sucking. One look and I'm captured, a slave to his whims.

"Tell me something sexy," I command, eager to distract him.

"You will stay," he says on cue. His hands encircle my waist possessively, tethering me to him. *Trapping* me with no hope of escape. "I will keep you here, beauty. You are mine."

I don't argue. Instead, I press my lips against his jaw and slide my hands down his chest, resting them over where I know his heart to be. "Be honest with me, and I won't be able to leave. So… Where were you?"

"Business," he says, brushing his lips over my forehead. "Though that's not everything. I…" He sighs, pulling back to face me directly. "This time of year is difficult for me."

"Oh?" Driven by the raw emotion in his voice, I force the lust to the back of my mind. "Tell me?"

He frowns. Then he stands, lifting me onto his desk. Stepping between my legs, he keeps me pinned in place, his captive audience.

"It's nearing the anniversary of…" Something in how his expression constricts makes me able to guess the answer.

"Your escape?" I say hesitantly when he doesn't explain.

He nods. "One day, I will tell you more. I swear to you. But…"

"I understand," I whisper, even though inside I'm torn. Could the mysterious Irina play a role in the pain of this anniversary? God, it's too selfish to consider, let alone mention out loud.

Instead, I settle against him, resting my mouth against the crook of his neck. Soon enough, I'm kissing my way down his collar bone, feeding off his startled—yet encouraging—grunt.

He claimed to have never had a relationship with a woman—but that's the scary part. Relationships could be categorized and forgotten. But true, rare connections went deeper than such a word. They were insidious, everlasting, even after the recipient of such feelings vanished.

They lingered, never disappearing.

And no one else could ever fill that void.

CHAPTER ELEVEN

The next morning, my wakeup call comes in the form of a contented sigh that fans across my shoulder in a burst of heat. I open my eyes to the man lying beside me, so beautiful in half-wakefulness that it hurts. Overnight, whatever had been bothering him seems to have vanished. His devious grin makes a triumphant return as I snuggle into him with a matching peaceful sigh.

"Morning," I murmur.

He strokes his fingers through my hair, marveling at the reddish strands. "Morning. A very good morning." He shifts, revealing a hardening erection that strains against my hip. I murmur in sympathy and slither beneath the covers to test just how rested he is.

Minutes later, he's fully awake, sitting on the side of the bed with a reluctant frown. "Early start today," he says before standing and heading into the bathroom. "I have some deliveries coming."

"Oh?" Though the logical part of my brain warns me against getting too excited, I can't help it. I sit up, licking my lips at the possibilities.

Until he rains on my parade with a stern frown. "None for you. Well, maybe one is for you, but please don't try to fuck it."

I laugh at his serious tone and scramble from the sheets to join him, standing naked before the shower as he washes down. I don't know who, between the two of us, is enjoying their view more. He groans like a man at his whit's end when he finally leaves the shower to find me leaning against the countertop, fondling my breasts.

"You'll be the death of me," he whispers, eyeing me from head to toe. Then he shakes his head, and I sense him struggle to contain at least some of his lust. Enough for him to escape into the bedroom without lunging for me. "I can't afford a delay today," he insists while scrambling into the closet. "Some of these deliveries are time-sensitive…"

He seems to lose his train of thought as I prance toward him, my hips swaying. I manage to steal a five second's detour worth of a kiss before he breaks away, cursing and snatches a shirt from a hanger as if it's armor against my charms.

"Please," he grates. "Give me this morning to be level-headed, and I promise I'll reward you later. After your punishment."

Satisfied, I get dressed beside him, and we venture downstairs to find the first of his "deliveries" already being carried across the foyer by a team of workers. Ena stands nearby, directing them with curt, one-word instructions.

"Vadim." I grasp his hand and stand on tiptoe to plant a kiss along his jaw. "She'll love it," I tell him.

He strokes my cheek in return, his gaze distant. I suspect he doubts that very statement, still stuck on her obvious hostility.

"Check on her for me?" he asks as if hesitant that I'll refuse.

"Of course." I risk teasing him with another quick peck, and then I head down the hall and cautiously enter Magda's room. She's still dead asleep, her tiny chest rising and falling with every soft breath. The semblance between her and her father doesn't end when they sleep. Though... Something about Magda's button nose makes her expression less tormented than Vadim's. More calculating. Even in slumber, it's like she's still thinking, still planning.

A trait of her mother's? It's a cruel thought that doesn't leave me as I circle the bed to stand in front of her, copying our positions from yesterday in reverse.

"Morning, sweetie," I say until she opens her eyes, frowning at the sight of me.

As if oblivious, I approach her window and pull back her curtains, letting in the fresh sunlight. Then I rummage through her end table until I find the wooden brush and climb onto the bed beside her.

"Which of your outfits shall you wear today?" I ask her, while extending the brush before daring to touch her. It's only when she doesn't cringe out of my reach that I gingerly stroke through her thick curls and smooth them into place. "The turquoise dress? I loved that one."

She doesn't say, choosing to crush It to her chest instead while she endures my brushing. Once I'm finished, I smooth her hair back and enter her closet in search of a headband. Ena—I'm starting to wonder if he may be more of a Saint than a devil—

somehow managed to not only unpack every purchase from yesterday, but he arranged them by color and even stocked a glass cabinet with every accessory. I strongly consider extending our truce as I pick out a black velvet headband and turn to find Magda behind me, observing her options with a frown.

In the end, she settles on the turquoise sweater dress with a pair of leather Mary Janes. The resulting look is too darn cute—a little princess, grumpy beneath the weight of her crown.

"I'm hungry," she declares afterward, tugging on my hand. While I marvel at the fact that she's touching me at all, she manages to drag me into the hallway. Downstairs, Vadim had the piano placed near the back of the living room by the window.

The second she spots it, her lips part into a smile she can't contain. "That's for me?" She runs over to the instrument and tentatively strokes the polished surface.

Vadim stands beside her, his expression slack with relief. "Yes," he says, stooping down beside her. "It's yours. I'm still arranging your lessons, but do you want to try it out now?"

She nods, and he lifts her onto the bench and settles down beside her.

I find myself inching closer, riveted as he begins to play a soft, jaunty melody before showing her where to place her fingers to achieve the same sound.

Single Father of the year. My ovaries swoon, but then a part of me resents that statement. *Taken* man of the year, it insists. *Mine.*

Rather than immediately quashing the thought, I get lost in their interactions, skipping ahead to imagine dangerous variations on this very scene. Me seated beside them, for one. Another child with his curls perched at his shoulder. Another. Another…

Snap out of it, Tiffy.

"I'll make us something to eat," I whisper, excusing myself into the kitchen. I rummage through the freezer and attempt to heat up one of Ena's meals. In the end, I get distracted and creep right back to the boundary with the living room.

But they're gone.

Confused, I search the rest of the lower level, finding it deserted. Did they leave? By the time the food is fully heated in the oven, they haven't returned. I fish out the container and divide the food between three plates. Just as I bring them to the table, a tiny figure races from nowhere, snatching for my hand.

"Magda? What's wrong?"

Her eyes are bug-wide, but all she does is tug until I warily follow her through the foyer, out the front door and around to the side of the house. There, at the end of the massive driveway, Vadim is unloading his latest delivery. At least now, his suggestion regarding my present takes on newer significance.

A gorgeous white mare nuzzles at his neck as he strokes her ivory mane.

"Will you welcome your new family members?" he asks, while enduring Zzazza's ruthless affections.

Magda looks on, spellbound, but when a worker guides another animal from the back of a white trailer, she releases me and races over.

"Is he mine?" she exclaims in response to the beautiful chestnut pony prancing at the end of a pink lead rope.

"*She* is," he says, reaching out to pat the small horse. "Her name is Dasha. Will you care for her with all of your heart?"

She nods solemnly and inches forward to touch the pony herself. As the filly sniffs her fingers, she smiles for real this time, completely unaware of the expression. And it's breathtaking.

"And for you." Vadim turns his attention to me, his voice lowering. "It took me a while to find a creature to fit your specifications. Does he suffice? His name is Magnus."

I gasp as a second worker leads another horse from the trailer. Majestic and completely ebony, he's the second most beautiful creature I've ever seen. The first watches me intently, gauging my reaction.

"He's incredible," I whisper, advancing toward the beautiful stallion. He watches me with lipid eyes, snorting as I extend my hand for him to smell. I can't even begin to imagine his cost, and the enormity of the gesture makes me sway.

"Shall we show them to their new home?" Vadim asks, speaking to Magda.

She nods, and together, they and the workers lead the horses down the path toward the stable. I watch them go, sensing the need to hang back this time. I can only pray that Vadim can continue to make progress without me. Still, my thoughts are solely focused on them as I return to the kitchen and continue setting the table. It seems, however, that a pony delivery may appeal to Magda more than chicken nuggets.

Sure enough, after an hour passes, I venture out to find them in the stable. Near the one apparently earmarked for Zzazza, Vadim holds Magda by her waist, high enough for her to brush the mare's ivory mane.

His eyes meet mine from over her head, brimming with a tenderness that warms my heart. I keep my distance until Magda spots me. It's like a switch is flipped, and being caught near Vadim is a slip in her façade she can't maintain. She wiggles from his grasp and backs away, crossing her arms.

"Can I ride my pony whenever I want to?"

Vadim frowns, and as if his hands mourn the loss of contact, he braces both against Zzazza's broad back. "You can with supervision," he says. "Either myself, or Mr. Ena. Horses are beautiful creatures, but they can be dangerous."

She nods and exits Zzazza's stall, extending the distance between them. And I know she has no clue as to the pain that slices through him like a knife. I can't stop myself from approaching his side and covering one of his hands with my own.

"Can I go to my room now?" Magda asks.

"Yes," Vadim rasps. "You can."

"Make sure you grab some lunch first before you head up," I call after her.

The second she's out of earshot, I loop my fingers around his neck, burying my face against his shoulder.

"I'm trying," he says hoarsely. I notice his hands withdraw from Zzazza and curl into fists. "Like hell, I'm trying. But I feel like she's putting up a wall every time I get somewhere."

"Give her time." I stroke my fingers down his front, sensing the muscle lurking beneath the tailored fabric. "I think you're wearing her down."

"I think I'm worn down." He captures my hand, bringing my fingers to his mouth. Our eyes meet as he brushes his lips over my knuckles. He eyes me reverently, like a man lying prone before an altar, desperate for mercy.

It's too darn intense. Awed, I stroke through his hair, driven to give him some kind of reassurance, even against my better judgment. "I'm here with you," I tell him. "I've got your back."

"Just my back?" His sly smirk makes me chuckle and arch into him, wrapping my arms around his neck.

"When do I get *my* day of special deliveries?"

"You've gotten them," he says cryptically, his gaze unreadable. "If you are a good girl, I'll let you unwrap them."

In the absence of prying eyes, I kiss him, groaning as his lips part against mine, and his tongue matches my own thrust for thrust. It feels so good, stealing these moments with him. I shamelessly tease the erection hardening beneath his slacks, but with a groan, he backs away.

"I would have you on the ground," he swears in a tone that makes my toes curl. "Naked beneath me. But—"

"With our luck, Magda would come skipping in," I finish for him. "I understand, Mr. Dad."

Chuckling, he takes my hand, and we return to the house together. Up above, a smattering of dark clouds thickens, promising a storm—the first drops of which start to fall the second we escape into the kitchen.

Magda's plate is missing from the three on the table, and Vadim and I eat in silence. He's brooding again, I suspect, stressing over her reaction to him. A reaction that confuses me the more I think about it. Apart from Maxim, Magda had been... challenging, fitting the term Ms. Anderson used, but when it comes to Vadim, it's as if she deliberately stops herself every time she starts to soften toward him.

Like she's *refusing* to soften toward him. Curious as to why, I place my dirty plate in the sink and head for the stairs. "I'll check on her."

In the hall, a strange haunting tune teases my ears, drifting from Magda's room. That foreign lullaby.

"That's beautiful," I say, finding her slumped on her bed while tossing the hapless It into the air. "Did you learn that at school? What language is that?"

She frowns and lets the bear fall onto the bedspread. "No." Rolling onto her knees, she eyes me warily as if deciding something on the spot. "Will you play with me?" Her defensive tone makes me suspect that it's a request she's used to having denied.

The Robinsons and their ineptitude strike again.

"Of course." I sink onto the bed beside her and kick out my legs. "What will we play?"

"Tea party," she says innocently. "I'll be the queen, and you'll be my loyal subject." She looks me dead in the eye as she adds. "And I'm going to poison you."

"You're supposed to be dead!" Magda shrieks in indignation, her cheeks pink. But her lips twitch, fighting a grin she ultimately succumbs to as I writhe, still in the midst of my "death throes."

"I *am* dead," I tell her mournfully. "Or maybe I'm not? Maybe I'll…" I shoot to my feet and lunge, my fingers drawn, aiming for her armpits. "I'll stage a coup and decide I'm the new queen!"

"N-No!" she exclaims between giggles. "You can't!"

We collapse into a heap, laughing hysterically before I even register how odd that fact is. She's laughing, batting at my hands as I tickle her ruthlessly. It's such a strange, unexpected moment. I can't explain what it feels like.

My shock must match Vadim's as he appears breathless in the doorway, presumably assuming the worst from Magda's high-pitched shrieks. "Are... Is everything okay?" he asks, his hair mussed, his suit ruffled.

Just like that, Magda falls silent and sits upright, her frown firmly in place. "I'm tired," she says.

Sure enough, the sky is darkening. We've spent almost a full day already though it feels like snippets of time.

"I've made dinner," Vadim says softly.

We follow him downstairs, and Magda makes a show of picking at the food on her plate, though in the end, she eats a majority of it. Then she heads back up to her room with Vadim and I hot on her heels.

"Do you want me to brush your hair?" I ask her, unable to resist tugging on the end of one curl as she climbs onto her bed.

She seems to hesitate. Then she shakes her head, her eyes on Vadim. "I'm not a baby."

"Okay." I stand and join Vadim, closing her door behind me.

"We'll be here if you need us," he says.

I can't stand his tormented expression as we head to the bedroom. Literally. The only way to salvage my selfish pain is to close the door, lock it, and boldly strip my dress as he watches. I saunter to him slowly as he backs up toward the bed and sits on the edge, waiting for me.

I straddle him and kiss him as deeply as I craved to in the stable. When he relaxes, I slide my hand down between us and grip the erection throbbing inside his slacks, freeing it. Sinking to my knees, I worship him, taking him into my mouth as deep as I can.

I relish in his groans and the reverent way he strokes my hair even while on the verge of pleasure. I'm so drugged on the moment, that I'm tempted to break my one last rule. Drawing back from him, I breathe against the pulsating head of his cock, watching his piercing jump.

"I could stay..."

Mayday. Too far! I look up in horrified anticipation of how he'll react. Gloriously. Like I said, the most beautiful, magical words in existence. Eyes glowing, he fists his fingers through my hair, guiding me up so that our lips meet.

"Again," he commands against my mouth in a tone radiating authority. "Tell me I can have you."

Too dangerous. Too...wrong. Right? We barely know each other. A few short weeks can't be enough time to breach such a raw, intimate boundary.

Not even if he's begging and desperate, his hollow eyes open, craving affection no matter how small. In this moment, I can't deny him. Not of a lie. Not anything.

"I'll stay," I whisper, brushing my lips over his once. The phrases he demanded I repeat while manacled on the bed return to the forefront of my mind, ample fodder to feed his pleasure. "You can have me. I desire you. You deserve—"

He shifts, trapping me beneath him, and I surrender to his thrusts as he slams inside me, moving in a brutal rhythm. The entire time, I continue to speak to him, my voice rasping, my thoughts scattering.

CHAPTER TWELVE

We collapse breathless and spent beneath the sheets. Before we even fully come down from the high, he's dragging me into his arms.

"Don't regret now," he warns, his tone gruff. "I know I need to earn those words. But hearing them? I will pay any price to hear you say them again."

"No price," I insist tiredly. "Just honesty." Something that's been on my mind all day chooses now—of all times—to resurface. "Why did you leave her, really? What made you think you couldn't take care of her?"

Just from how he interacts with her, his nurturing instinct is wholly intact. Something deeper must have shaken his confidence. A hint as to what shapes his expression now—raw, unbearable pain.

"My real surname isn't Gorgoshev," he admits—an unsurprising admission given his accent. "My mother never gave me one, and my father denied me his... I was worthless, a bastard unworthy of belonging to any family. I never envisioned starting one of my own."

I brace my hand over his forearm, my throat tight. No man should sound so depreciating—especially not him. So beautiful, so intelligent. Can't he see that?

No, I suspect, reading his stricken gaze. He can't. He's blind to that aspect of himself entirely.

"Back when… In my captivity," he says hoarsely, "we had no say over our clients, mind you. I'll let you interpret that statement as you may. Reading people became a strict criterion for survival. I was adept at it. Until one day, a man came before me who wasn't like the others. He had been promised a luxurious getaway on my employer's estate—which in reality was a setup to frame him, allowing my employer to use his presence there as blackmail. This man was a professor, and a researcher in a prominent biotechnical company. His knowledge and skillset made him a tempting target for those in the realm of garnering black-market information. In pharmaceuticals. Genetics. Biotechnology. You'd be surprised the price such knowledge can fetch."

I listen to him in silence, my heart throbbing at his clinical, detached tone. He almost sounds like he's reading from a script, not recalling his own past in chilling detail.

"The man's name was Hiram Gorgoshev," he says. "And rather than utilize his power to abuse me, he saw through my act. We were well trained, you see, expected to lie to our clients, creating the façade that we were willing participants rather than the victims we were. Slave owners, you see, cringe in abject horror when faced with their victim's chains—but as long as they're hidden out of sight, they can sleep at night." Real emotion colors his tone—disgust. Rage. Hatred so searing, I flinch as if burned.

Reflexively, he grips me tighter, preventing me from pulling away, even if I wanted to.

"Hiram *saw* me," he says. "He spent his time with me reciting the laws of physics rather than refuse outright and risk having me beaten. He sacrificed his own leverage just to ensure that. I didn't understand the risk he took back then. I had no idea…" A rare, broken smile shapes his lips for a fleeting moment. "He even offered to help me escape—but I couldn't. Not then."

My brain mulls obsessively over his potential reasons why. For Irina?

"When he finally did leave, he slipped a piece of paper into my hand with an address on it," he explains. "But it wasn't until a year later that I finally gained my freedom."

"And you went there?" I ask, craning my neck to better see his face.

He nods. "I wound up before a modest estate in Germany, wearing rags, my mental state in ruins. I think at that point, Ena had to force-feed me bits of bread during the trip, or I would have died from starvation by then. When Hiram saw me, shivering on his doorstep, he brought me into his garden. Gave me a cup of tea. He offered his home to me so that I could rest… And I don't think I left once for six whole months." A muscle in his jaw twitches, and he strokes the flesh with the tips of his fingers. "And that entire time, he kept me fed. Clothed. He let me heal my fractured psyche, and when I was ready to reenter society, he gave me his name. More than that. He used his connections to get me a world-class education more comprehensive than what the children of some dignitaries are privy to. He guided me to a prominent position in his own company, Eingel Industries, which was a fledging, but promising, venture. When the time came, he ceded control to me, and even when my wealth far surpassed his, never did he ever ask me for anything. Not once. I think… He was the closest thing I've ever had to a father." He sounds confused, even as he says it. As though it's a realization he's only *just* come to. "He was the one who helped me navigate Magdalene's sudden appearance," he adds. "Nothing ever caught him off-guard, not even her existence. He encouraged me to gain custody of her, in fact. When she was sick, he was preparing to come on the next flight from Munich just to see her. That bear she has? That came from him. His idea anyway. But in the middle of her illness, he died suddenly of a heart attack, and I couldn't even leave her side to go mourn him."

"That's why you dedicated the garden, the one at your building," I say, my eyes widening as everything clicks into place. "For him. It's your way of saying goodbye… I'm so sorry."

"Maybe it worked out for the best." He shrugs. "I wasn't ready then."

But for some reason, I doubt that he truly believes that. Maybe it's just easier for him to reconcile it.

But the reminder of his vigil over her bedside triggers a thought I can't seem to suppress. "When Magda was sick… Did you ever sing to her?"

He frowns, lowering his mouth to my forehead. "That is a strange question to ask after sex."

I have to croak out a laugh at that. "I'm serious. Humor me. Did you?"

He purses his lips, thinking it over. Then he nods. "Yes. I think I sang to her. Some silly song about a group of hens. It was the only thing to come to mind—"

"Was it in French?" When he raises an eyebrow, I add, "Sing it to me?"

He sighs, but slowly, his voice forms the words of a lilting melody. He sounds rougher, and reluctant, but I can barely smother the shock dawning on me like a blow. It's the same song.

"Satisfied?" Vadim asks playfully when he finishes. "Though I will admit that in terms of ways you might seek to exploit my devotion, forcing my humiliation via song was fairly low on my list."

"You said she was on a ventilator," I say, referring to Magda. "But was she awake at all? Is there any way she could have heard you?"

His expression darkens. "No. She was in a medically induced coma. The moment she regained consciousness, I left."

"But you were there for days," I point out.

He nods. "Over a week. Day and night. She wasn't placed with a family then, so I could pull the right strings to have access. Why are you asking this?"

I bite my lip, torn between telling him my suspicion or staying silent. It's a stretch, yes. But so is the fact that a seven-year-old who's only grown up in America could know the same obscure French melody about "a group of hens" sung perfectly in tune to his halting rendition. Though...

As much as it stings to admit, she could have learned the song from anywhere.

"What made you sing that to her?" I ask him. "Why *that* song?"

His eyes go distant, and I fear I might have gone too far. Softly, he says, "My mother used to sing it to me. I was so young… I have no idea how I've remembered it. As for why? I don't know. What else could I do? I read to her, sang to her, recited the laws of physics as Hiram did for me… And yet I couldn't even face her the moment she got well. I ran. I left her. What good is a fucking song now?"

He releases me and rolls onto his side with his back to me. "Goodnight."

I nestle into him, melding against his rigid contour even as he stiffens against me. I stroke my fingers down his forearm, finding his hand and capturing it. Then I settle my mouth against the crook of his neck and inhale him deeply.

"I think it meant more to her than you know," I tell him. "Your presence meant more to her. I think that you don't need to spend thousands on ponies or pianos to buy her affection. You have it. But she's as stubborn as you are. Trust that she'll come around. I think you're connected to her, more than you know. She feels it too."

In fact, I suspect that Magda may know far more than she's led him to believe…

If he feels the same, he doesn't admit as much out loud. Maybe it's easier for him to ignore the small, subtle signs?

I let him have this one victory and remain silent. God knows he's earned it.

I DON'T KNOW what startles me awake. Just that I wind up blinking through the darkness as Vadim stirs beside me.

"Did you hear that?" he asks, his voice sharp with concern.

It's enough to make me shrug off exhaustion entirely and sit upright. Together, we strain through the silence until…

"Magda!" He lunges from the bed, stopping only to grab a pair of boxers before peeling into the hall. I follow him, snatching a robe for myself. The further I go, the more apparent the sound becomes—sobbing.

Magda's. She's huddled beneath her blankets, her face buried in the crook of her arm.

"*Ma chérie*," Vadim murmurs, switching on her light. He crosses to the bed and crouches down, stroking her hair until she faces him. "*Qu'est-ce qui ne va pas?* What's wrong?"

Redness paints Magda's cheeks, and I can almost see the battle within herself. To recoil from him even as a part of her is lulled by his soothing tone. There's no denying his concern. No ignoring the fact that he would do anything in this moment to help. She can't resist.

"It," she says, though she looks at me as she does so. "I lost him. I think he's out there." She points to the window where a flash of lightning illuminates the landscape, making her flinch.

"Is that all?" Vadim stands. "Stay with her," he tells me as he enters the hall.

Sighing, I sit on the bed beside her. She lets me pet her hair, and I try not to notice as she inches closer to my side. It might break the spell. Together we wait as the storm rages beyond the window until finally, heavy footsteps ascend the steps, and a soaking wet Vadim reappears.

"Is this what you were looking for?" he asks, brandishing a relatively dry It by one of his floppy arms.

Magda sniffs and reaches for him, swiping away any lingering tears with the back of her hand. She cradles the bear to her chest, and Vadim's expression softens in a way I've never seen. Hopeful.

At least until she catches him staring and flings the bear violently across the room.

"I don't want him anymore." She burrows beneath the blankets, drawing them over her head. "Can you get out, please?"

"Yes…" Vadim retreats, his expression stricken.

I remain behind just long enough to switch off the light, but as I close the door behind me, I notice a tiny figure crawl from the bed and dart across the room for a small object that she crushes to her chest.

These two will be the death of me.

When I reenter the bedroom, Vadim is sitting on the edge of the bed, his face in his hands. Eyeing me through his fingers, he exhales an exhausted chuckle. "What was that about her softening to me?"

I sigh in sympathy and join him, leaning against his shoulder. "I need to ask you another seemingly pointless question."

He grunts. "Oh?"

"How did you explain the bear?" It's a weird question on the surface, but not so weird when her attitude toward him is taken into context. I know firsthand that she has other stuffed animals she has yet to mutilate. But that one she vandalized. *That* one she carries with her everywhere. The only one she sleeps with at night and panics if she's without.

"I'm sure they told her it was donated by a nurse," he says offhandedly.

But what if she already knew that it hadn't been? What if that one bear mattered to her so much because she knew its original source. And through that very same bear, she loved tormenting said source.

"We should get some sleep." I crawl up the mattress and slip beneath the covers. "I need you well rested for tomorrow."

"Tomorrow?" Vadim wonders as he follows me, snatching me into his arms.

"Yes," I say, arching into his touch. "Magda needs some toys. You're taking us shopping."

CHAPTER THIRTEEN

Put a shopaholic and a shopper-lite into any Boutique in the fashion district with an unlimited credit card, and chaos will ensue. Put a man desperate to buy his daughter's affections into a toy store—a man with no concept of money or boundaries—and watch as they fall into a silent power struggle that I'll be lucky to survive without getting slung across a cash register myself.

By the time Magda makes her way toward the store's extensive doll section, I feel compelled to put my foot down.

"She doesn't need one of every doll, Vadim," I scold.

Following dutifully in her wake, he eyes me the way I figure a kicked puppy might, and I march forward, prepared to put him out of his misery.

"Magda." I crouch down beside her and meet her calculating gaze. She's wearing a burgundy ensemble that enhances her eyes to an almost painful degree. With her curls held at bay by a matching headband, she looks every bit the little princess she must think she is. The only flaw in the façade is that battered, deflated teddy bear clutched to her chest. "I want you to get something you really want. Something you'll play with every day."

She frowns, mulling over the request. But as I hoped, she seems to take it as a challenge rather than a demand.

"That one." She points to a particular doll high up on a shelf. Behind me, I sense Vadim already scrambling to find a salesclerk to retrieve it. It's one of those porcelain frilly dolls decorated in an ivory Victorian-style costume with a straw bonnet and huge reddish curls.

Vadim pays for it on the spot and removes it from the box, handing it to her. I watch in awe as her lips part into one of those rare, incredible grins. Meeting my gaze, she says sweetly, "I'm going to call her *Biphany*." She pats the doll's head lovingly, shoving her bonnet down her face in the process. "She's an orphan, poisoned by the queen. And everyone hates her."

"Magda…" Vadim sounds horrified.

I, however, raise an eyebrow. "Is that the best you can do when it comes to a backstory?" I feign a yawn and rise to my full height. "Boring. I bet you can come up with something better."

She pouts, the gears in her brain ever whirling.

When we finally leave the store—with about only half of it in tow—Vadim takes us out for lunch, where Magda makes a show of refusing anything from the menu he suggests to her. In the end, she winds up drinking only a milkshake, and pointedly ignores him for the rest of the trip.

It's taking its toll. His usual enduring patience wears thin. His eyes turn hollow and distant. When we return to the house, he lingers in the garage to carry the bags while Magda marches inside, It slung under one arm and Biphany under the other.

I follow her into the foyer and watch her dump her toys on the lid of the piano before climbing onto the bench.

"Why are you needling him?" I do my best to sound as nonjudgmental as possible. I'm not angry with her. Just curious.

She taps a piano key, letting the note play out. "Because," she says, just as heavy footsteps approach from the direction of the garage. Her head cocked, she whirls around and meets my gaze directly. "I hate him."

A heavy thud draws my attention to the corner of the foyer, where Vadim stands amid a pile of fallen shopping bags. As I watch, his wall comes up too quickly to stop. His eyes darken, his expression rigid. Without a word, he gathers up the bags and carries them upstairs.

I watch him, my heart aching. I almost start after him, but tiny arms go around my waist, keeping me in place.

"I like *you*," Magda says, her face in my hip. "You don't lie like other grown-ups." She draws back and snatches my hand, tugging me after her. "Can we go see my pony?"

"Okay." I follow her, my heart in my throat. We venture out to the stable and spend time brushing down Zzazza and the other horses under the watchful eye of Ena, who appears from nowhere to stare from the shadows—on his master's orders, I suspect.

"Can I ride?" Magda asks as we approach Dasha's stall.

"You could ask Mr. Vadim to teach you?" I suggest, hopefully.

She gives me a look that sums up her thoughts even before she utters a terse, "Never mind."

We settle for cooing over Dasha from afar. When we return to the house, an incredible smell reaches my nostrils the second we step inside.

"Don't tell me you've decided to add chef to your list of accomplishments," I exclaim in response to the sight of Vadim standing before the counter amid a variety of vegetables and ingredients in various states of preparation.

"Have a seat," he says without turning around. "Name your drink preferences, both of you."

"Wine for me," I blurt, alarmed as he turns around, his expression blank. Is he still hurt by Magda's hostility? *Yes.* I can see the hurt coloring his irises, but he's smothering that pain for her sake.

Turning his attention to the tiny figure climbing onto a stool beside me, he tentatively asks, "And for you?"

She frowns. "Orange juice."

"As you wish." After fulfilling our drink orders, he continues to cook, filling the room with incredible smells, while I attempt to prod what little information I can from Magda.

"What do you like to do with your friends?" I ask in between fortifying sips of wine.

She folds her hands with It perched on one side of her, and Biphany on the other.

"I don't have friends," she says. Her surly tone could betray the words as yet another lie meant to provoke, but her eyes tell a different story. A hint of vulnerability creeps through that unnerving blue and something in my heart throbs, rubbed raw. "I don't *need* friends," she adds firmly, rephrasing it.

"What about hobbies?" I ask. "Do you have any of those? Do you like to read? Play games?"

She strokes her chin and nods with sudden seriousness. "I like to plan world domination." *Damn.* She utters that declaration without even a hint of mocking inflection.

"Oh, goody!" Feigning nonchalance, I clap my hands together. "Then, to get started on your merry way, you need to beat me at the one game perfect for world domination training."

She eyes me skeptically. "What game?"

I wink and rise from the table to approach the lone figure slipping in through the glass door leading out to the terrace. Ena eyes me the way I figure one might either a hungry lion advancing toward them or a diseased rodent.

Writing it off for the greater good, I lean near his ear and make one whispered request.

I can't tell from his surly expression just how he processes it. Finally, he nods. "I be back."

I watch him scuttle off, utterly pleased with myself. I'm even more pleased by the results Vadim comes up with when he finally leaves the kitchen to adorn the dining table with platters of steaming, amazing looking food.

"Fresh vegetables, salad, and homemade garden burgers," he declares, indicating each platter with a wave of his hand. "Let's eat."

One bite, and I groan in appreciation. "This tastes incredible."

Even Magda seems impressed enough to endure his physical nearness as she samples a burger with delicate bites. By the time we finish the meal, and Vadim has cleared the table, Ena arrives as if on cue, brandishing my sole request.

Barely suppressing a grin, I rise to my feet and accept what turns out to be a rectangular board game infamous among my family's gatherings.

"You aim for world domination?" I ask Magda. "Let's see what you've got, kid. Try your hand at the ultimate decider."

I slam the game board onto the table as Magda and Vadim share puzzled looks.

"Monopoly?" He reads from the gameboard lid as though he's never played.

And I'm alarmed to realize that he might not have. Neither of them may have.

"You poor innocent fools," I tell them mournfully. "Prepare to have your butts kicked by the real estate queen."

CHAPTER FOURTEEN

An hour later, I realize that, though untested in the ways of Monopoly they may be, both Vadim and Magda are fearsome opponents. I wind up going bankrupt early on, and the game quickly shapes up to be a brutal war between their two growing fictional conglomerates.

"I think you're a sore loser," Vadim remarks in response to my pouting. In the same breath, he completes his purchase of yet another block of hotels, extending the reach of his empire.

"Am not," I hiss in indignation while fulfilling my new role as banker. "I'm just hoping that Magda kicks your butt and keeps your ego firmly in check."

As if to rise to the challenge, Magda promptly proceeds to buy out an entire strip. I'm so impressed I ruffle her curls and beam at Vadim. "Long may she reign! Can you defeat the queen?"

What unfolds next is a long, hard-fought battle, but in the end, Vadim concedes with a groan while I shower Magda in a flurry of paper money. Her tiny lips twitch, resisting a smile that gradually unfurls despite her best attempts to squash it. And her pride only seems to grow as Vadim stands and bows to her grandly.

"Your majesty." He extends his hand to her. After a brief moment of hesitation, she places her small fingers over his, allowing him to help her stand on her chair while we continue to shower her with accolades.

"What do you wish to claim as your prize?" Vadim asks her, his eyes gleaming.

Magda doesn't seem to need even a second to think it over. "Can you teach me to ride my pony tomorrow?"

If possible, Vadim's eyes glow, brimming with hope. "As you wish."

It's a moment so real, so very genuine. I don't think my heart can contain it, and I start to play that dangerous game. Wishing. For more. For him. Them. This.

Stop it, Tiffy.

My only hope is that something happens to shatter this moment before it becomes too potent to ignore. But in a cruel twist of fate—coming in the form of advancing footsteps—I get my wish tenfold.

Vadim reacts first, his expression darkening as I turn to find Ena marching into the kitchen with a taller figure in tow.

"Mr. Hood," he announces gruffly. "He come. Already cleared."

Apparently, Milton doesn't require the same security reserved for Maxim. His expression wary, the British man steps forward, dressed in a gunmetal-gray suit and a blood-red tie. His dark eyes go directly to Magda, widening as he takes her in.

But she pales and nearly falls off the chair in her scramble to get down. She winds up jumping, but rather than onto the floor, she flings herself at Vadim, who catches her seemingly by instinct, holding her close.

She copies the same stance she took in the presence of Maxim—her face buried against his shoulder, her knuckles white as she grips him tightly.

But this time, Vadim strokes her back with a sigh. "It's okay, *ma chérie*. This is…Uncle Milton." His voice conveys nothing but soothing warmth though his eyes tell a different tale. He looks like a man who came close to claiming a pile of gold, only to have it slip through his grasp at the last minute. And he eyes Milton as though he's the force that made said fortune vanish.

Unperturbed, the other man boldly steps forward. Almost before my eyes, it's as though he transforms, softening the harder, angular stance of his rigid posture for a softer, friendly appearance. Even I'm fooled, almost forgetting the imposing figure he so regularly presents as. Smiling warmly, he says, "You must be Magdalene. I'm a friend of your… Mr. Vadim's."

Sensing the danger has passed, Magda squirms from Vadim's arms and scrambles away from him, her cheeks pink. She eyes Milton warily but doesn't move to take the hand he extends her way.

Without missing a beat, he uses the same hand to reach into the breast pocket of his suit jacket and withdraws an enormous lollipop even the surliest child couldn't resist. Case and point, Magda steps forward, and he crouches on one knee and presents his offering to her.

"Sugar-free, of course," Milton declares, glancing at Vadim.

Magda takes it and eagerly rips off the wrapping, before taking a tentative lick. Her eyes practically light up even as she takes a step back from him. I watch in awe as she reaches out with her free hand, finding Vadim's pantleg. Their expressions mirror each other's for a split second—hers irritated by her seemingly overwhelming need to cling to him, while he seems overwhelmed all at once.

Rising to his feet, Milton maintains his polite, charming smile, but when his eyes meet Vadim's, something unspoken flashes between them. It's like I can sense the atmosphere shift in an instant.

"It was very nice to meet you, Magdalene," Milton says. "But right now, I'd like to borrow Vadim for a minute."

Vadim glances at Magda, and I can see the internal struggle as he wrestles with leaving her. But then he cuts his gaze to the other man. Again, some understanding flashes between them and his jaw clenches. Sighing, he captures the hand Magdalene has on his pant leg, and I can tell that nothing in the world pains him more than having to ease her away.

"I'll be back," he swears, stepping forward. "And I will bring you a reward fit for a conquering queen."

Whether the promise mollifies Magda or not, I can't tell. She's utterly stoic, watching as the two men head toward the study. I skip toward her, and I can't resist tugging on a dark curl even though she wrinkles her nose and turns away.

"Help me clean up, oh majesty?" I ask her before eyeing the fortune of fake money scattered over the floor.

She eyes me skeptically, crossing her arms. "Queens don't clean up."

"Hmm." I stroke my chin and nod. "Not normally. But they do if the treasury is at stake and a thief is on the loose, threatening their fiscal hold on the populous!"

I stoop for a fistful of money. Alarmed, Magda drops to her knees and attempts to grab as many bills as she can before I snatch them first. Within minutes, we've gathered up every last bit.

"I win," Magda declares as she places her haul back into the box.

I can't resist tugging on another curl though this time she doesn't seem to resist. "You did! Awesome job…"

I trail off, distracted by a sudden noise coming from the hall near the study. Angry, thumping, brutal noise. Smiling wider for Magda's benefit, I playfully tap the bridge of her nose with my finger. "Why don't you figure out how to set up for a second round, oh majesty? I'm going to go grab a pen so we can keep score."

I use that harmless lie as my excuse for tiptoeing down the hall. Not the urge to spy or eavesdrop. I need a pen. A pen that ceases to matter completely the second I catch Vadim's grated rasp.

"…and you still seem to hold out hope that we will reconcile?" he laughs. "I don't think so. Not after this."

"You did provoke him," Milton replies, his tone level. "You know how he can get. Like a dog with a bloody bone. Give him time to cool down."

"Time?" Vadim echoes coldly. "Don't play coy, Milton. You aren't a gossip, and you wouldn't be telling me of his little ultimatum if you didn't believe he was serious in this threat. What was it again? 'I leave within three days, or he will take *measures*.'" He laughs in that icy, beautiful way that resembles how I figure a fallen angel might. One seriously considering joining the ranks of Lucifer. "And you asked me why he will never see Magdalene?"

"Like I said, give him time to cool down," Milton insists. "Besides, he'll be gone for a few days. He's on his way to Moscow. Apparently, *someone* disrupted a supply chain of munitions he had stored there. Damn near took out an entire arm of his operation overnight. You wouldn't know anything about that, would you?"

Munitions? Supply chain? Something at the back of my brain tingles, filing away those terms for later. They sound far more sinister than the typical business venture, that's for damn sure.

"Would you be surprised if I did?" Vadim asks dryly. Gathering up the nerve, I creep forward enough to peek into the office through the cracked door. He's leaning over his desk, his eyes downcast.

Milton must be standing before him, his posture rigid. "No. Especially not after you accused him of disrupting your own business interests there—an accusation he denied, by the way. And you know he wouldn't shy away from claiming ownership if he had."

"Or maybe you've just grown too damn trusting," Vadim counters with a harsh laugh. "Would you believe me if I denied it? Perhaps a part of me gets some sick pleasure out of making little Maxi squirm?"

I shiver at the coldness in his tone. But just as quickly, his posture seems to slump, his body deflated.

"I've humored Maxim's hostility far longer than I should have," he says softly. "But I am telling you now, Milton. If he dares to do anything, I won't be so forgiving this time."

"He's all bluster," Milton says. "Between the shit going on in Russia and the shock of discovering your little secret, you might want to cut the man some slack. I will admit that I was skeptical at first myself. That you were planning one of your little mind games to drive the man insane. But, damn... She looks just like you." His voice deepens, conveying the depth of his awe.

"Which is why..." Vadim sighs. "Maxim can harbor his hatred toward me all he likes, but I will *never* let him hurt her—"

"And I would?" Milton counters, stepping forward to brace his hands over the desk. "Threatening children isn't Maxim's style, you know this. But I will suggest you consider moving anyway. Why provoke him further?"

"Why?" Vadim shakes his head, chuckling to himself. "You always take his side. I've ceded this city to Maxim for ten years. I've dwelt in the shadows and let him play king. Not anymore. I said it once, and I will say it again—I'm taking what I want. For myself and Magdalene. Her desire is my only concern, so if he wants to get in my way, let him try."

"Or," Milton says softly, "you two could finally put aside your petty feud and play happy families. Especially if you both are so intent on starting your own."

"Don't compare me to him." Vadim stands and turns his attention to the door just as I manage to scuttle away.

I find Magda seated at the dining table with a neatly arranged and reset monopoly board before her and a look of utter ferocity on her face.

"Ready for round two?" I ask, joining her with a forced grin.

She kicks my ass. In the end, I have to concede with shreds of my pride left intact.

"You are well on your way to world domination," I tell her as we clean up the game for good. "But I'm still the adult, and I will always have one superpower over you, even when you rule the world."

She raises an eyebrow. "What's that?"

"Bedtime."

I follow her upstairs and into her room, where I enter her closet. "I'll pick out your pajamas while you take your bath, okay?"

Surprisingly, she doesn't argue. Minutes later, she's dripping wet and freshly dressed in a pair of ivory silk pajamas that make her resemble a dark-haired variation of the porcelain doll tucked under her arm.

"Can I brush your hair?" I ask, moving toward her end table as I speak.

After a moment's hesitation, she nods and climbs beneath the covers while I sit beside her and tackle those gorgeous curls. This time, I deliberately ignore that warning voice telling me to back away. That I shouldn't be enjoying this. Smoothing my fingers through her hair shouldn't feel this natural, neither should I take pride in how she relaxes against me.

I'm not her mother. It's wrong.

"I thought you might be asleep..."

I look over to find Vadim hovering in the doorway. His eyebrow raises as he spots me beside Magda, and I smooth one last curl into place before backing away. She's already slumped against the pillow, her eyes drifting shut. When she spots what Vadim holds in his hands, however, she bolts upright.

"I thought you might need this if you are to ride your pony tomorrow," he says, stepping forward to place a large, white box on the bed. It's wrapped neatly with a turquoise ribbon that Magda rips off before lifting the lid.

Her mouth drops open, and I can't smother a grin as she gingerly withdraws a sheet of tissue paper to reveal a pair of tan jodhpurs, a white riding blouse, and an ebony jacket, complete with a riding helmet.

"They're beautiful," I murmur as Magda runs her fingers over the material.

Though she doesn't admit it out loud, I can guess from her wide-eyed expression that she feels the same.

"I'll let you get some sleep," Vadim says, seemingly not expecting much more gratitude from her than that. "Goodnight."

My heart feels swollen as he leaves. I slip from the bed and make the mistake of looking back. Magda's already slumping sideways, her eyes falling shut even as she clutches the sleeve of her new jacket. I lift the box from her bed and set it aside before gently easing her beneath the blankets. I tell myself that the act is purely out of necessity—but brushing a stray curl behind her ear isn't.

Neither is making sure that both Biphany and It are within her reach before turning off the light and finally leaving her room.

The panic I feel is ten times stronger than the emotions I try to resist when it comes to Vadim. I've had my heart stomped on by a man before. As much as it stings, I can survive that pain again. But I don't think there's a cure for loving a child that isn't mine.

Don't do this to yourself, Tiffy.

I enter the master suite and find Vadim sitting on the bed as if waiting for me. He's removed his suit jacket, and the topmost buttons of his dress shirt are undone, revealing a tempting sliver of his chest. It's a fitting distraction from budding emotional turmoil. After locking the door behind me, I eagerly start to strip my dress.

"Wait." He stands and crosses to me. I've rarely seen him so tired, his lips pursed, eyes unreadable. Alarmed, I let my hands fall from the skirt of my dress as he captures each one, stroking the knuckles. "You are...incredible," he tells me.

But this confession feels different from his prior attempts at practicing praise. His voice reaches down into some secretive, innermost part of me, making it bloom despite myself. Swell. I feel my cheeks catch fire, my throat tightening. The feeling has nothing to do with selfish pride or gratitude—it's far simpler than that. It's a desperation I've been struggling to ignore. A desperation to feel useful to him. To help him. To make him feel safe enough to keep his wall down around me, even as I mutter something about needing to leave. Boundaries.

"*You* are incredible," I tell him, inching closer. I bury my nose into the crook of his shoulder, inhaling him as his arms encircle me, cradling me to his lean frame. I've never felt so safe before.

And so very exposed.

A FLURRY of commotion has me blinking my eyes open to a darkened room, my heart racing. Shadows flicker along the walls, cast by a quickly moving figure darting from the closet. Before the panic can crest, I recognize that surly frown, barely visible through the dark.

"Vadim?" My voice croaks, heavy with sleep. "What's going on?"

"Go back to sleep." I stiffen at the steel in his tone. He marches back into the closet, and I hear hangers clanging together. The clock on his nightstand reads that it's barely six a.m.

"You're leaving?" I murmur as he stumbles back into the room, wrenching on a pair of loafers.

His gaze cuts up to mine, constricted with visible torment. "I… I need to attend to something. Get some sleep—" He crosses to me, brushing his lips over my cheek in a hasty kiss. "I'll be back later today. If you need anything, I'll have Ena stay close by."

His wary grin struggles to convey a calmness that his stiff posture contradicts. Once he wrestles on his suit jacket and loops a tie into place, he practically races from the room.

Alone, I slump against the pillows, but it's impossible to fall back asleep. Eventually, I slip into a robe and head downstairs in a futile search for coffee. Vadim, it seems, is a tea man. After heating up a kettle on the stove, I make myself a cup of some fancy French blend I can't even begin to pronounce. Then I sit at the dining room table and watch the sunrise sluggishly over the water, my thoughts in turmoil.

To distract from his absence—and all the many potential causes for it—I scan the view beyond the window glass, pleasantly surprised.

Vadim's been making small improvements to the property day by day, it seems. The playground is nearly done, lacking only a completed swing set. Near the water, I can see that the docks now sport two small rowboats that instantly make me imagine lazy days on the water beside him, Magda in tow.

A dangerous fantasy to indulge for sure. One that seems more impossible to attain when tiny footsteps allude to the figure who prances into the kitchen.

The second I see Magda decked out in her riding outfit, my heart breaks. I can barely muster up the strength to meet her gaze, especially as her lips part into a rare, fleeting grin.

"Can we ride my pony now?" she asks. Her eyes excitedly scan the kitchen, presumably for Vadim. And my heart splinters all over again for them both.

"He had to go away on business, honey," I say thickly. "I'm sorry."

As if she inherited his internal emotional switch, her expression falls and hardens in a way that triggers a horrible sense of *déjà vu*. Just like Vadim, she knows how to erect a wall in a heartbeat, closing herself off.

"He'll take you as soon as he comes back," I insist, rising to my feet. "I promise."

But he won't be back anytime soon, I suspect—though I don't have the heart to say it out loud. I saw it in his face. The pain of being away from her, even for a short amount of time. Whatever drew him away, might keep him all day again.

And something tells me that Magda knows that as well as I do. She spins on her heel, racing from the kitchen.

"Honey, wait!" I follow her up the stairs, wincing as the door slams in my face. I test the handle, finding it unlocked, but when I finally push the door open, she's lying face down on her bed.

Her shoulders shake though she's overall silent. Her pale skin reddens, and I imagine her biting her lip as hard as she can to keep any noise inside.

"I'm so sorry, honey." I sit on the edge of the bed and tentatively place my hand on her back. "I know you're disappointed—"

"I'm not!" She wrenches away from me and snatches the helmet off her head, throwing it across the room. Then she glares at me, her expression so fierce I suck in a breath.

Until, she breaks. Before my eyes, she transforms from a mini, ice-cold Vadim into a seven-year-old girl whose hopes have been dashed. Tears spill from her eyes, and I can't stop myself from snatching her into my arms. Boundaries be damned, I hold her even as she squirms until finally, she succumbs, sobbing openly against my shoulder.

"I know, honey. I know…" Helpless, I can only smooth my fingers down her back, letting her cry. A part of me suspects that this emotion has nothing to do with her pony and everything to do with something deeper. Something that makes her melt into my embrace, too exhausted to fight. I rock her, speaking reassurances that I doubt she even hears.

Eventually, I coax her into pulling back enough for me to see her face.

"How about we go pet your pony?" I suggest, wiping away some of her tears.

Her eyes blaze. "No!" She lunges from the bed, storming into a corner, her arms crossed.

"Okay." Sighing, I start to follow her only to change tact and enter her closet. "Let's go for a walk instead, hmm?" I take my time picking out the clothing I suspect were her favorites from our shopping trip. The red dress. The black faux fur stole. It doesn't matter if they're too extravagant, I help her dress in them as she allows me to stiffly manipulate her limbs, her expression blank.

I gingerly brush her hair and arrange her curls behind a red headband. Then I take her hand and lead her downstairs for a quick snack before we step out onto the terrace. It's a relatively beautiful day, though the sun is hiding behind a screen of overcast. Still, it's warm enough out, and a gentle breeze enhances the natural beauty of the property.

"Do you want to swim?" I ask, pointing to the pool.

Magda shakes her head, her wall still in place. She doesn't even show interest when I take her past the partially done playground and suggest she try out the jungle gym. It's only when we near the water's rocky edge—where a grunting Ena is adjusting the docked rowboats—that any semblance of curiosity shapes her otherwise flat expression.

Like a shark sensing blood, I latch onto the potential diversion. "Would you like to see if we can go out onto the water?"

After a second, she nods, and I nearly drag her over to Ena.

Forcing what I hope passes for a charming smile, I try to meet his gaze as he wrestles with a length of rope, securing it to a post on the dock.

"Mr. Vadim gone," he says gruffly before I can say a word. "All day."

"Do you think you could take us out?" I ask. I have to physically stop myself from batting my eyelashes in the hopes of cajoling a yes.

His lips part to deliver what I suspect is an automatic no. But then he makes the mistake of looking at Magda and something in his surly expression cracks.

"Okay." He sets his rope aside and lumbers into the boathouse, returning with two orange life vests. "You put on." He shoves the preserver at me but stoops into a crouch and takes his time assisting Magda. She stiffens, but gradually submits to his surprisingly gentle instruction.

The moment we're sufficiently dressed, Ena steps into one of the boats and helps us down from the dock. Taking up both oars, he sets us off while I settle in beside Magda.

That logical, nagging part of my brain picks up again, warning me against letting her sit too close—I don't move. But I should pull away when she nestles into me, shivering against the cooler air over the water. I shift an inch, putting space between us only to put my arm around her a heartbeat later. That little act of rebellion is the gateway drug to crossing even more boundaries. I smooth back her fluttering curls and stroke away one of the final tears as her expression brightens.

Even Ena seems to fall under her spell, and he keeps his pace steady, steering farther out into the bay. Eventually, her blank mask cracks, revealing genuine excitement beneath as she scans the shores and gentle roving waves.

She sits forward so suddenly the boat jolts beneath us. "Look!" She points to a spot along the left-hand beach. There, up on a ridge, appears a little white pony with a flowing mane. Riding him is a small girl with blond hair streaming from an ebony riding helmet. Spotting us, she waves, and to my surprise, Magda offers up a tentative one in return.

"It looks like you might have a friend to play with after all," I blurt. Only to feel the color drain from my face as a woman appears beside the girl, holding the pony's reins. She's slender, with long brunette hair, but even from this distance, I recognize her instantly.

Maxim's fiancée.

Ena too must sense the property he's unintentionally strayed into. Grunting with the effort, he immediately begins to turn the boat around.

"Can I play with her?" Magda tugs on my arm, and I can tell from her surly expression that she doesn't like to beg. Because that's what she's doing—begging. "Huh? Do you know where she lives? I bet I can find it!" She starts counting on her fingers, her lips moving wordlessly.

"Oh, honey…" I tuck a curl behind her ear, wrestling with indecision. In the end, my feelings match Ena's. "Let's go get some lunch, huh?"

Magda's frown returns, lasting the entire trip back to the house. When we enter the kitchen, I do my best to feign supreme excitement in finding something to eat amongst Ena's prepared meals. "How about some pizza, hmm?"

I fish out the meal and pop it in the oven while she watches me from the counter.

"Can I go wait upstairs until it's ready?" she asks.

I nod, relieved to leave the topic of our possible neighbors behind. "Go ahead. I'll get you when it's ready."

She scampers off while I set the table and fish some fresh orange juice from the fridge. Ena must stock it regularly, maintaining a methodical sense of order with just a few bare things he needs to keep Vadim, and now Magdalene, alive. It's such a contrast from my old fridge in the home I shared with Jim, when I had it stuffed with failed attempts at baking and cooking. All because he insisted I play the role of the perfect housewife.

He'd scoff in disgust if I ever had the nerve to serve him a previously frozen meal. The thought makes me frown. It's been at least a few days since I've thought of him. Why now? In an effort to distract myself, I rearrange one of the cupboards, moving around Vadim's already neatly composed collection of glass dishes. Then I grab the food from the oven and head upstairs to get Magda.

"Come and eat, it smells divine…" I push open her door only to find her room empty. So is her bathroom and the closet, and she isn't in the hallway. "Magda?" I check the master bedroom but don't find her there either. Returning downstairs, I scan the kitchen and the living room only to come up short.

My heart is starting to race, my palms slick with sweat. A barrage of worst-case scenarios crosses my mind as I race out onto the terrace and check the pool. Thank God, she's not there, but neither is she anywhere within view. A harsher sense of dread thickens my throat as I run to the dock. I'm almost too horrified to scan the water at first.

But…

The boats are still here, as are the lifejackets left inside the one we took out. I don't see any sign of a tiny body floating on the water. I'm so relieved that I have to bend over, bracing my hands over my knees. And then I hear it—faint, soft laughter, riding a gust of wind.

Out here with little noise on the property, sound travels far. Blindly, I plunge beneath the trees, following the laughter through brambles and faded trails for what feels like an eternity.

"Magda?" My heart is a constant hammering pulse by now. I feel like I might vomit, and a call to 911 is my next course of action until I spot a tiny flash of scarlet between two trees. "Magda!"

I throw myself into the underbrush and crash out on the other side.

"Oh, thank God!"

Magdalene stands just a few paces away, her red dress wrinkled, her shoes muddied. Otherwise, she looks none too worse for wear—as does the blond girl standing beside her. Both watch me, wide-eyed in a way that makes me question my own appearance. I'm panting, my skin slick with sweat.

"Sweetie, don't you ever take off like that again! I was worried sick! And I'm sure your mother is worried about you too," I tell the girl.

Magda shrugs, her tiny lips pursing. "Can I visit her pony?" she asks. After a moment's hesitation, she adds, "Please?"

"Yeah!" The little girl pitches in. She's beautiful—the blond equivalent to Magda's dark-haired visage. Her tiny riding habit is secured by a bright pink ribbon, the fabric every bit as expensive as the one Vadim bought Magda. Something tells me that despite their feud, the two brothers share the same inclination when it comes to spoiling the children under their protection. "My house is right over there," the girl adds, pointing through the woods. "We can play whenever we want!"

"Ainsley!" In a scene that I assume must mirror my appearance just seconds ago, a woman staggers from a copse of trees. "Don't you ever run off like that. I—" She breaks off, her brown eyes flitting in my direction.

Again, I'm struck by just how young she is. Especially when paired with a man like Maxim, who—while no old man by any means—is certainly far older. And stronger. And bigger. I'm so lost in the mental comparisons that I barely notice when she speaks.

"Ainsley, come back to the house."

"And we should be leaving too." I step forward and take Magda's hand. Surprisingly, she doesn't resist.

Instead, she turns her eyes on me, deploying an as of yet unseen ability—puppy dog eyes brimming with as much intensity as her trademark icy glare.

"Can she come over to play? And see my pony? …please?"

"I, um…" I make eye contact with Maxim's fiancée. Francesca, I think that's her name. Without a word spoken, I sense that we share a mutual understanding—these children may be innocent in the affairs of the adults around them, but it's better not to touch that dynamic with a ten-foot pole. "We'll talk about it later, sweetie. Come on, your lunch is getting cold. Maybe after we can go pet Dasha, hmm?"

She follows as I tug her along, but cranes her head back to watch as Francesca does the same to Ainsley. The two girls wave at each other while my insides squirm uncomfortably. How utterly cruel is it to deny a child a potential playmate merely because their guardians hate each other?

Very, I decide once we return to the house, and Magda's frown makes a dramatic reappearance. I cajole her into eating, and we're in the middle of another game of Monopoly when the front door opens. I turn only to choke on my relieved sigh; Vadim isn't the one who storms into the kitchen.

"Mr. Vadim no come back," Ena declares. "Business. Be back tomorrow."

"Tomorrow?" I try to keep the panic from my voice. "Can I call him? Do you have his number—"

"No call." Ena crosses his arms, and I have enough sense to suspect that point is non-negotiable. "He busy. You see him tomorrow."

"But what about…" I trail off, glancing at Magda. This isn't her fault. I can discuss the whole "how dare you abandon me with your child" issue with Vadim at a later date. Instead, I force a grin and pick up the dice. "Ready to get your butt kicked, kiddo?"

She smirks, apparently more than eager to accept the challenge.

CHAPTER FIFTEEN

I figure I should be far more pissed at becoming a forced babysitter than I actually am. Because that's what this is, isn't it? Babysitting?

Because, as I've told myself repeatedly, Magda isn't *mine*. I shouldn't enjoy losing to her at Monopoly for the umpteenth time. I shouldn't find an odd sense of pride in the fact that she allows me to pick out her pajamas—a pink, gossamer nightgown —while she takes her bath. Brushing her hair is far too personal a task for a glorified babysitter, as is tucking her in and ensuring that both of her dolls are within reach.

"Goodnight, sweetie."

I return to Vadim's room alone, finding the bed huge without him here. And as I huddle beneath the silken sheets, a wave of doubt crashes over me with such brutal intensity, I almost can't breathe beneath the onslaught. Where is he? Is he safe? Or has something happened? Something that drove him off on one of those emotional benders he's hinted at?

I spend the night tossing and turning as those various fears torment me, robbing any anger I should feel of potency. I'm exhausted by the time I finally crawl out of the still-empty bed and get dressed. Downstairs, I make myself more tea and turn my sole focus to Magda.

Pushing any thoughts of boundaries aside, I make her a bowl of cereal for breakfast and pour her a fresh glass of juice. Then I head upstairs, relieved to find her still in bed.

Perched on the end of her mattress, I run my fingers through her hair until she wakes up. "Time to get the day started, kiddo."

Rubbing her eyes, she sits up and scuttles to the end of her bed, waiting expectantly. It's a belated second before I realize why. Following my unspoken cue, I enter her closet and pick out another outfit—a pair of jeans and a lime green sweater. After I braid her hair, she follows me downstairs and eats.

Then she fixes me with another disarmingly vulnerable glance I'm woefully unprepared for. "Can I go play with Ainsley?" Her eyes are so wide I feel swallowed by them, devoured by their openly pleading nature. "Please?"

I fumble for my glass of juice and promptly knock it over. "I… Um, we should wait for Vadim to get back." I force a grin, but her mouth falls flat in response. From her dour expression, I assume that she feels the same way on that prospect that I do deep down—who knows when that will be?

"I want to play," she says, folding her hands beside her bowl.

It's such a simple, plaintive statement that somehow slips through my defenses and cuts deep. Maybe because it's a different tact from her stoic persona. I'm just as vulnerable to her as I am to Vadim when he lets his true emotions slip through. Helpless.

"I… I'll be right back."

My mind spins as I leave the kitchen and head aimlessly for the foyer. Instead of Vadim returning, I find Ena standing guard, his arms crossed as I approach. And a split-second's decision forms in my brain too quickly to challenge.

"I want to make a deal," I tell him as he eyes me warily. "And I know you'll want to refuse it, but hear me out."

He cocks his head, his frown skeptical. "I listen."

"Magda wants to play with the little girl next door—" As far as mansions with acres of property go. "And I think she could. And yes, I am talking about Maxim's daughter."

Ena's nostrils flare, and I almost take a step back. He looks liable to hit me, revealing the true depths of his loyalty to Vadim. "No. No—"

"I'll take all responsibility," I insist, lifting my hands in a placating gesture. "Or… I'll tell Vadim that you let her wander onto his property unprotected. I found her there yesterday."

It's a low blow. One I would never resort to under different circumstances. Is a playdate even worth it?

No. Ena's furious expression warns me that making an enemy out of him is the worst possible act I could have taken.

"Look at her," I demand, trying another tack. "She's cooped up in a strange house, with strange people. The man who brought her here just disappeared to only God knows where. She's lonely. All she wants to do is play with a little girl her own age. Are you going to tell her no?"

He squares his jaw, and I have no doubt that he's capable of doing just that. He takes a step toward her, only to deflate, his shoulders slumping. Whirling on his heel, he jabs a finger at me.

"You take blame," he insists. "Ena knows nothing. You take girl on your own."

I sigh in relief. "Thank you—"

"No thank me." He laughs coldly, his upper lip quirked. But it's not a smug expression. It's pitying. "Mr. Vadim kill you."

And he may, I concede to myself. But not if I kill him first.

"Thank you." I race past Ena before he can change his mind and approach Magda. Any doubts I may have are instantly dashed when she gazes up at me, her wall lowered a fraction to reveal the little girl underneath.

Screw boundaries. If Vadim wants to leave me with his daughter overnight, then he would cede her to my authority. Gosh, I just hope that trust isn't misplaced.

"Ready to go on an adventure?" I run upstairs just to grab a jacket from the closet, then I open the door to the terrace and lead her outside. Taking her hand, I let her show me the route she took the other day.

"How did you even know where to go?" I ask, already hopelessly confused by the vast expanse of nature rendering this section of the grounds a virtual wilderness.

"Nautical navigation," she says, a rare hint of excitement seeping into her voice. She has Biphany clutched under one arm, but curiously it looks like she left It behind.

"Oh," I say, nodding. "Nautical navigation... Which in English means?"

She giggles in that rare, fleeting way. "Like the pirates used," she adds in response to my puzzled expression. Lifting her tiny fingers, she points in two opposing directions. "Longitude and latitude—the lines that go on a map like this. Then you use the position of the sun—" she points up above. "And cardinal directions, you know—east, west, north, south. You use those to estimate your position on the axis. Then you just calculate from there. If I assume that we were fifty feet out on the water, then Ainsley lives roughly..." She counts on the fingers of her free hand. "One point seven five miles west of our house. See? It's easy." Whatever expression she sees on my face makes her giggle, shaking her head. "It's basic calculations. Even a baby could do it."

"Yeah," I say, almost stunned into silence. "Basic..."

Still grinning, she surges ahead, tugging me behind her, and all I can do is follow, seeing the world as a seven-year-old might. An exceptionally bright seven-year-old who is far too perceptive for her own good. Vadim and Maxim may have a proverbial ocean of emotional distance between them, but a child has no trouble cutting through the physical boundaries. Which isn't much. Once upon a time, these properties were connected, it seems, linked by a series of dirt paths that are now barely visible in the underbrush.

And yet, as a testament to the vastness of both properties, Maxim's is still a good twenty or thirty minutes' walk at the brisk pace of an eager seven-year-old. If Maxim is anything like Vadim in terms of security, I half-expect a gruff, gun-toting equivalent of Ena to come bursting from the shadows the second we breach the boundary of his land. Instead, we emerge from the woods relatively unscathed—though I sense eyes on the back of my neck with every step we take toward the modest, cozy-looking mansion on the hill.

Maxim's property is laid out much in the same way as Vadim's. There is a stable on the far edge, set amongst a series of sprawling, fenced-in fields. Beyond that is a rocky shore with its own private dock. The house even has a pool, barely visible from this angle.

Inhaling deeply, I take Magda around the perimeter of the property, heading toward the house proper. The second we step onto a paved stone path snaking to the front door, it opens, and a man in a suit steps out. He's dapper, with graying hair and gentle though guarded eyes. I recognize him instantly as the man who drove me home after Vadim made a spectacle of me at Maxim's dinner party.

Small world.

"May I help you?" he asks, smiling warmly. The politeness catches me off guard, and some of my unease dissipates a fraction.

But before I can open my mouth, Magda steps forward. "I want to play," she says. "Is Ainsley here, sir?"

I gape at her even as my heart melts at her sweet tone. Like father like daughter. She knows when to turn on the charm. It doesn't hurt that even in her more casual outfit, she still looks like a little princess with her braids adorned with green ribbon and Biphany tucked under her arm—I now suspect that leaving the less innocent-looking It at home was a calculated choice.

One that turns out to be devastatingly effective. The man blinks at the overload of girlish energy. But in a testament to his professionalism, he doesn't break completely.

"I'm not sure if Ms. Ainsley will be able to play today," he says carefully, cutting his gaze to me. "But I will ask."

He disappears inside the house, and not even a second later, the door flies open, and a tiny figure skips out.

"You came!" Ainsley bounds down the path, sporting a pink equivalent to Magda's casual sweater and jeans. Her loose hair flows over her shoulders as she bounds toward us. "Can we go play, Frankie? Huh?"

She directs the question toward the slender figure who appears in the doorway behind her. Cautiously, the woman's dark eyes meet mine, and I sigh in response.

"Can we talk?" I ask her as the girls ignore us, already skipping off together, holding hands. Their innocent joy makes it painfully apparent just how foolish this is—the adults being nervous at the prospect of a budding friendship merely because of two men who hate each other. It's laughable in theory. But not so trivial once I recall how the brothers react when in the same vicinity.

I feel like a general, going behind her leader's back to forge a truce behind enemy lines. Yes, on the one hand, every small ounce of peace is a victory within itself. On the other hand, treason is punishable by death, and even Ena didn't care to sugar coat things.

Mr. Vadim kill you.

But the time for any doubt has sadly passed. Tentatively stepping forward, Francesca nods, and I suspect she's of the same mind. In unison, we watch the girls giggle, muttering conspiratorially, and any lingering misgivings I may have held vanish.

"Come on, Ainsley," Francesca calls, her expression strained. "Let's go into the back yard."

IT IS a strange thing to sip lemonade behind enemy lines for the sake of a playdate. I add the experience to the growing list of *"things I thought I'd never do during my journey to sexual exploration."*

Stoically, Francesca sits beside me on a wooden lounger while we both watch the girls play on a section of grass across from a spacious pool. Here, the similarities between Maxim and Vadim's properties end. Maxim's is lived in, for one—a landscape of toys and skateboards bustling with activity. I catch several other faces peering out from the windows at times.

"I know this puts you in an awkward spot," I say to break the ice as Magda and Ainsley chatter away. "But when you have a seven-year-old stuck in the house for a week, it gets hard to deny her request for human interaction. And she's so darn cute." I crack a smile.

And so does my opponent. She really is beautiful in an understated way, with curling dark hair and brown eyes. *Haunted* eyes. A black dress with short sleeves reveals the bare skin of her arms—a sight I am desperately preventing myself from staring at.

They're covered in scars. Vicious, healed scars.

"You live with Dima?" she asks, her tone surprisingly neutral, given the nature of this war.

"Dima?" It takes me a second to remember Vadim's nickname. "I, um… Yes. For now. It's complicated."

Her lips form a wry frown. I sense her mulling over her next words carefully before she finally says, "He's dangerous."

I swallow at her tone. My gaze cuts to Ainsley, who seems merrily undisturbed, though, according to Maxim, Vadim kidnapped her. It's a horrible act for sure, and while I don't claim to know Vadim fully just yet—I *do* know him enough to understand why he might have done it. To test himself. To convince himself that he could interact with Magda. He all but told me, and I don't doubt that looking back at all he's done since.

"He's…complicated," I say in answer to Francesca's statement. "I won't pretend like he's not."

And hell, after today I may not have to—he'll kick me out. I try to feel more guilty, but as I watch Magda smile as she shows off Biphany, my heart swells up so big that there isn't room for any other emotion but relief.

"Complicated is one way to put it," Francesca says, her eyes narrowed in a way that makes me suspect she hasn't forgiven him. Not one damn bit.

"I know what he did was awful," I confess. "To Ainsley. I hope it didn't traumatize her, I truly do. But maybe Maxim should take a page from his book the next time he breaks into our home and terrorizes a little girl."

Oops, I realize as her eyes go wide. It seems Maxim didn't tell her that little detail.

"Dima brings out the worst in him," she says, her lips pursed. It's not an explanation—I don't think it's meant to be one. Not really.

It mirrors something Vadim told me once himself. These brothers, so hostile, and yet so damn similar. Will they ever be able to let go of whatever hatred is simmering between them?

"I think it's stupid that two little girls can't play because their fathers are insane," I blurt out loud.

Francesca eyes me for a moment. Slowly her small smile returns. "Maxim isn't her father," she says. "She's not even mine. She's my sister."

"Ah." I nod, and some of the uncomfortable tension between us eases. "Well, Magda's not mine, either."

Though you seem to think she is, a part of me hisses. *You're making decisions for her after all, behind her father's back.*

"But she's Vadim's, isn't she?" Francesca says with a sureness that alludes to the fact she too can see the resemblance. "I'm sorry, but he doesn't seem like the fatherly type."

"He's trying," I admit with a sigh. "He really is… I take it, you aren't his biggest fan, though?"

She bites her lip as if to stop herself from saying more. Then she shrugs. "I don't like being the recipient of his little mind games, that's for damn sure."

Yikes. I file away that assertion for later. Could Vadim be manipulative? Yes, case and point is my current predicament— despite all my insistence to the contrary, I'm watching his daughter while he gallivants off to only God knows where. But are said actions malicious? Francesca seems to think so.

She stares off into the distance, frowning as if at an unpleasant memory.

To change the subject, I blurt out the first thing that comes to mind. "Are you excited for your wedding?" It's the wrong topic, one I'm woefully unable to be objective about. To my own horror, judgment leeches into my voice, far too potent to go unnoticed. "I got married young," I confess apologetically. "It didn't end well. I'm a bit jaded about it. Please allow me to live vicariously through you, though."

Francesca eyes me warily, an eyebrow raised. "We haven't planned much," she admits.

From her tone, I suspect it's not by choice. Could the delay have something to do with whatever drew Maxim to Moscow? Rather than pry, I shrug.

"I remember my own wedding. I put so much effort into it, when I should have put more time and energy into planning my future, sans some self-centered asshole."

Ouch, Tiffy. This isn't about you. Once again, Jim rears his ugly head, and I don't know why. Why the hell would I bring up marriage at all? But my lips rebel against my brain, carrying on the conversation, "I *was* too young," I add, eyeing the woman up and down. "Twenty, barely out of high school. I had no clue. Not that there's anything wrong with getting married young, that is..."

Judging from the faint pink coloring Francesca's cheeks, she's not too far from the twenty-year age mark. Damn. I could kick myself for insinuating something so rude. "I'm sorry—"

"Don't be. I'm not ashamed of my relationship with Maxim," she says with a maturity that puts past Tiffy's mindset to shame. Her eyes take on that faraway look, betraying a difficult past I can only speculate on. "He's not perfect. I'm not either. But I don't have to justify that to anyone."

I tilt my glass, finding far more solidarity in her words than I care to admit to myself at the moment. "I'll drink to that."

We finish off our glasses, still watching the girls. They chase each other, each one cackling madly as if in a competition to prove who is having more of a blast. If mirth could be graded on the decibel scale, then I'll say this is one hell of a successful playdate.

"Ains doesn't really have anyone her age to play with outside of school," Francesca says after a moment's silence. Her voice is so soft, it's almost as if she's talking more to herself than to me. But that seemingly harmless statement opens the door to so much more.

And for Magda's sake, I step right on through. "We're just next door," I say carefully.

But we both leave it at that without crossing over that unspoken boundary.

Not yet.

CHAPTER SIXTEEN

Magda and I return to the house under the disapproving glare of Ena, who skulks off the second we're safely inside. Vadim hasn't returned yet, it seems. Sighing, I fix Magda a pre-prepared meal, and then we spar in another round of Monopoly.

Much to my utter joy, I don't get slaughtered minutes in. That little play date must have zapped Magda of her energy because I'm seconds away from beating her when the door opens. My body shivers in recognition of those slow, heavy footsteps before Vadim even appears in the doorway.

I gasp, alarmed at his appearance. Any irritation for his disappearance vanishes, and I lurch to my feet, staggering toward him. He's paler than ever, his features gaunt in a way that makes me suspect he might have gone both days without eating. His hair is mussed, his suit wrinkled, and those eyes wretchedly hollow. They flit over me with barely any recognition before latching onto Magda. He barrels past me, snatching her from her chair despite her shrieked protests.

Sinking into a crouch, he holds her to his chest, smoothing his hands through her hair.

No matter how she struggles or resists, he doesn't let her go, his body trembling with tension. Eventually, she goes stiff with shock, enduring the contact.

"Vadim?" Alarm runs through me when he doesn't even react to the sound of my voice. I step forward, bracing my hand on his back—he's practically vibrating. "Vadim, what's wrong?"

He says nothing, so intent on Magda that I doubt he even heard me. It's only when she squirms against his grip that he finally lets her go. He stands as she darts across the kitchen and turns to me. Seconds later, I'm in his arms, his mouth capturing mine with a ferocity that leaves me breathless.

I arch into the kiss before common sense makes me draw back. "Wait. Baby, wait—"

He backs away, panting, swiping at his mouth. He blinks as if he's only now realizing where he is. Then he turns and heads for the stairs.

Shaken, all I can do is grasp at the pieces of the gameboard with trembling fingers. Magda watches me, her expression unguarded for once. She looks terrified.

Forcing a smile, I grasp a handful of fake money. "Let's clean up, shall we?"

She nods, her eyes still wide. Together we pack up the pieces and put the game away in silence.

"Why don't you go brush Biphany's hair, and I'll come to get you ready for bed, huh?" I force another grin that Magda doesn't return as she obediently heads upstairs.

Alone, I attempt to gather up the nerve to follow after her and approach the master bedroom. Vadim sits on the bed, his jacket on the floor, his dress shirt partially unbuttoned. As I approach, he meets my gaze, seeming more exhausted than ever.

"Are you okay?" I ask.

He glances away, running his fingers through his hair. "I'm fine. I'm sorry if I startled you."

"You are *not* fine." I stalk toward him and finger his wrinkled collar. My nostrils flare with his scent—all male musk. I doubt he's even showered since he left. "You look awful." I run my fingers through his hair, forcing him to look at me. "Tell me what's wrong."

His throat works to swallow. "I—"

"I'm ready for bed," a small voice declares. Startled, I lurch away from Vadim and turn to find Magda in the doorway her arms crossed, wall firmly in place. "Are you coming, *Tiffany?*"

"Yes... I'm coming, honey."

She nods and then pointedly glances at Vadim, her expression icy. Turning on her heel, she marches away, making her thoughts on his return abundantly clear.

"Damn it," he hisses, bracing both hands on his knees. He slumps forward, the picture of guilt, and some more of my irritation is chipped away. "The pony. I forgot..."

"I'll go put her to bed," I say, heading down the hall. "But when I come back, we need to talk."

I find Magda waiting for me on the edge of her bed. As I enter her closet to pick out a set of pajamas, I sense the unlikely start of a routine. One in which I return with her clothing and arrange it on the bed while she takes her bath. When she emerges dripping wet and draped in a robe, I brush her hair and braid it. Finally, I let her crawl beneath the blankets and tuck her in, placing her toys on either side of her.

"Night, sweetie." I linger far too long, smoothing my fingers over her hair until she finally drifts off. When I return to Vadim, he's pacing, still partially undressed, his expression even more constricted.

"I've fucked up," he declares the second I see his face. "She's angry with me."

"Yes," I say, choosing not to lie. "You disappointed her. And I'll tell you now that you'll have to work hard to make it up to her. No more just buying her things. Spend the day with her. That's what she wants—no, that's what she *needs* from you."

He sighs, his lips twisting into a frown. "And you are angry with me as well…"

"Pissed off, actually." I prance past him and lift my dress over my head, but I know my posture warns him from touching me. I am angry. I just didn't realize how strongly until now.

"I don't know what misconceptions you have, but I am not your employee," I tell him, my voice shaking. "You don't get to disappear and leave me with your henchman and your kid without even asking me to stay. You don't have that right, fake wife or otherwise."

"I know." I sense him come up behind me. When his fingers brush my sides, I don't pull away, leaning into him instead. Two days alone create an unfair disadvantage as far as maintaining a grudge is concerned. Luckily for me, I have one powerful bit of ammo in my holster. Best to get it out of the way now. "Before Ena spills the beans, I took Magda to play with Maxim's little girl."

He sucks in a breath, backing away from me. "You what?"

I swallow hard before facing him. Meeting his gaze, I square my chin—but it's a hard-fought bravery to keep up. I sway as his eyes touch on a terrifying shade of black. Soulless and cold at the threat of betrayal.

"You gamble her safety to punish me?"

"No! Of course not!" I scoff, insulted by the accusation. "I gambled your stupid pride and let your lonely daughter have some fresh air and play with a girl her own age because her father broke her heart over some stupid pony!"

He grunts as if struck, his gaze pained. I almost feel guilty for going there. Almost.

But if he wants to play the self-righteous indignation game, I can be just as petty. "Why did you go running off anyway? After how you made Magda feel, you better have one damn good reason—"

"I do." He's facing away from me, his tone hoarse. "I filed to adopt her the day she came here. The Robinsons had expressed no interest, and as her only previous foster family, I was assured that no one else could lay claim. I did everything in my power to expedite it legally."

I bite my lip. Could that explain his disappearance the other day on that mysterious "business?"

"So, what happened?" I ask. Something in his stance draws me to him. I place my hand on his forearm and gasp. He's trembling. "Vadim, tell me."

"My petition stalled. Blocked, in fact, though the reasoning why was unclear. My lawyers assured me they could have the hold-up dealt with swiftly… But the other day, I learned the real obstacle barring me."

He turns around, his expression shaped by such pain… I step into him, caressing the stern line of his jaw. I give him time to speak, sensing that whatever he means to say is hard for him to put into words.

"The person who blocked the adoption did so on the grounds of claiming to be Magda's biological mother."

"What?" My eyes go wide as a million implications come crashing down all at once. *Irina? Some other mysterious woman?* Overwhelmed, I stagger to the bed and sit down. "Is it the truth? C-can they prove it?"

"I don't know." He sits beside me and takes my hand, gripping it tightly. "I spent two days in the state of her birth, trying to learn the answers to those very questions. With all the fucking legal hurdles, I didn't get anywhere. But unless the petitioner comes forward and files in person, they still have no claim."

"But it's still a hurdle," I croak, panic constricting my throat. God, it's like what happened at my church all over again. An adoption ruined on a selfish whim—but not my own. Right? Wrong. Even after a few short days… "Could it be her?" I ask, my voice breaking. "Magda's mother? …Irina?"

He glances at me sharply, his eyes flashing with a million emotions ranging from suspicion to…resignation? I sense the bricks of his wall shifting, fighting to reform. At the last second, they fall, leaving his emotions accessible, as volatile as they are.

"So, you *did* hear," he says softly. "I don't know if it's her. But… She wasn't well back then—" He frowns at the memory as his grip on my hand grows firmer by the second, tightening to the point of pain. It takes everything I have not to pull away, for his sake. Lost among the shadows of his past, I sense he needs physical contact now more than ever.

"I wasn't either. You don't understand what it's like. I can't explain. But, if this is her, she isn't hiding out of shame I can tell you that. The girl I knew, she was broken. In her world, everything was a game. She needed that mindset, but I indulged her. Too much, I indulged her. If I had the choice, I'd pray to whatever God would listen that Magda *isn't* hers."

I swallow thickly. There goes my jealousy, at least, though I'm not sure if I like the emotion that replaces it. Fear? I listen to him ramble, hopelessly confused—but I don't have the heart to prod for more. This seems to be the only way he can explain this at all —in disjointed bursts of information with little context sprinkled in between.

"Could it be her?" He shakes his head slowly. "Who knows."

"But why not come see her? Why not visit her first? And if they aren't her mother, who would be so cruel?"

"I don't know," Vadim insists. "But one thing could strengthen my claim over her, biological mother or not."

"You mean claim that you're her father to the courts?"

"No. Something even better." He draws my hand to his mouth, planting a kiss over the knuckles. His eyes practically glow as they meet mine, brimming with conviction. Alarm bells go off at the back of my mind, even as my body heats in response to the naked passion conveyed in that one, searing glance.

Damn. I half-expect my clothing to melt, reduced to ashes by his desire alone.

"If I can prove that I can provide a stable home for her, no one could take her away," he says carefully. "And, if you join my adoption petition. Marry me for real..."

Mental overload. It's too much seriousness at one time. My brain can't cope. All I can do is laugh, pulling my hand away as I lurch to my feet.

"We could ask Maxim to make his wedding a double," I suggest, laughing. "His fiancée said they haven't planned much. I'm sure they'd be down for it."

I'm smiling, but as the seconds tick by, he doesn't return it.

"I would marry you in tandem with whoever you wanted," he swears in a voice that robs my lungs of air. "As long as you said yes."

I sway, stunned. He sounds too damn serious. Too convinced in the madness of his plan.

"Vadim... You don't even know me."

"I know enough to know I'm not making a rash decision," he insists, rising to his height, stepping into me. "I know that you care for Magda already. I know she's warming to you more than she ever might to me. I know I need you. And...I know that you care for me as well."

My cheeks flame. I can't even deny it. My only course of action is to parry his passion with logic. "So, you railroad me into another marriage without even feigning the guise of love first? At least

Jim gave me that." I don't know why I'm so angry. Because I am. Angry and hurt and torn by his dilemma. Could I even refuse him in these circumstances? That's the scary part. I'm not sure I can. "You should have told me what was going on sooner," I insist, changing tact to something I feel more comfortable punishing him over. "I could have comforted you. I could have understood why you left, and I could have helped you smooth things over with Magdalene."

"I'm telling you now." His voice is sin, soothing through my frustration like a salve. Too fast. I'm melting into him before he even touches me, his hands finding my breasts, kneading them possessively. "And I am not looking to 'railroad' you. As always, when it comes to you, I'm being greedy. Shameless. You want love? What about *need*? I always need more of you."

"Smooth talker," I rasp. It's alarming how he always manages to say the right thing. Even as my brain struggles to counter him with logic. The more he touches me, the less my fears make sense. The world narrows to this—him and me. My body heats, my hips writhing shamelessly to soothe the ache building between my legs. A heat that catches fire as my piercing remains rigid against swelling flesh, applying incredible pressure.

"Will you kick me out of your bed tonight as punishment for aggravating you?" he wonders. His lips find the crook of my throat, pressing there in a teasing kiss. Then a harder, teasing bite. "Or can I find some way to make it up to you?"

Damn…

"I think you're heading in the right direction," I gasp as his hands skim down my hips, finding my thighs. I spread my legs, encouraging him to travel lower. A gasp rips from my throat as his fingers slip between my legs, teasing the very edge of my piercing. My eyelids flutter, and I'm leaning into him, relying on his support just to stay upright.

"Mmm, my beauty. Don't tell me you've neglected yourself while I've been gone?"

Neglected… My brain spins, dizzy at the thought of fingering myself thinking of him. I hadn't. Why? "You didn't leave your toy for me," I confess. "I don't like to tease myself when I know waiting for the real deal will feel so much better."

He murmurs his approval, sliding a finger between my folds, tempting me with the promise of fullness. I spin around to face him, snatching at his collar. Logic can wait. He's right—I need this. Him. All of him.

Desperate, I rub my hips shamelessly against his thigh, teasing a groan from his throat.

"Still so insatiable…" He guides me backward, letting me fall onto the mattress. I spread my legs for him, gasping as he cups me, encouraging me rock against his palm.

"You find pleasure in this?" he whispers as my eyes threaten to roll.

His voice does something to me, triggering an avalanche of emotions, too overwhelming to resist. My lips part, the truth spilling out before I can stop myself, "I find pleasure in *you*."

"Prove it," he murmurs, nuzzling my neck, nipping intermittently with his teeth. "Show me how badly you crave this."

He bucks his hips, letting his cock graze my inner thigh.

How much do I crave him? Enough to lose my mind. Enough to forget my boundaries.

Enough to lose myself.

Enough to drown.

CHAPTER SEVENTEEN

I wake up utterly content. Rolling onto my back, I open my eyes to a room filled with sunshine and the pleasant weight of Vadim's arm over my waist. I nestle into him, so relaxed that I almost miss the tiny figure standing at the end of our bed, watching us.

Puzzled, I blink, but the intruder doesn't disappear. In fact…

As my brain wakes up, more of her expression comes into painfully sharp focus.

"M-Magda!" I lurch upright, clutching the sheet over my front. Beside me, Vadim stirs, still asleep. "What is it, honey?"

She frowns, crossing her arms over her nightgown, her glare accusatory. "You didn't wake me up."

"Huh?" I glance at the clock, surprised to find that it's nearly noon. Though, after last night, it honestly is no shock. Even Vadim's still out. Turning to Magda, I can't escape a wave of guilt as every real-world concern comes slamming back to the forefront. Her supposed mother. Her father's demands. The fact that I'm naked.

"Did you eat breakfast yet?" I ask her, clutching the sheet even tighter.

She shakes her head, and I scramble to the edge of the mattress. "Let me get dressed, and I'll make you something to eat."

The second she leaves, I dart into the bathroom and change in record time. When I scramble into Magda's room, she's still wearing her pajamas. After muscling her into the bathroom, I lay out a fresh set of clothing on her bed. Only then do I stop to realize what I'm doing.

Coddling her? Or maybe there's a worse word for it in this context...

Mothering her.

Mrs. Robinson eat your heart out. It seems the busybody was wrong about Magdalene in more ways than one. Though...she *was* independent her first few days here, dressing without prompting. I sense this new insistence on having me assist her has nothing to do with laziness. Oh God, I think it's deeper than that. More terrifying than that.

Did the Robinsons ever attempt to do this for her? Did the mother even try to tuck her in and lay out her clothing? Something tells me no. Am I making a huge mistake by letting her get accustomed to this? To me?

"I can't wear that without pants," Magda says from the doorway of her bathroom, seemingly amused by the fact that I've only placed a yellow cashmere sweater on her bed and nothing else. She giggles—a sound so rare and fleeting that I promptly squash my doubts and force a grin.

"Right you are, smarty pants. But let's try a skirt today instead?" I pick out a tan tweed one and a baby blue headband. Once dressed, she hops onto the end of the bed, and I heed my cue, settling in to brush and braid her hair, securing it with a length of yellow ribbon.

Downstairs, I make her a bowl of cereal and warm up a piece of toast for Vadim, who stumbles downstairs not long after. I can tell that he showered, throwing on a pair of sweats in lieu of a suit. Looking beautifully dazed, he rakes his fingers through his damp hair, and once again, his thoughts are easier to read than ever. Like the fact that he's alarmed for one, unnerved at having slept for so long.

"Your food, good sir." I place a plate in front of him and feel my toes curl at the gracious look he shoots me. *Damn.* Boundaries are important—if only he didn't make domestic life so damn appealing to imitate.

But weddings can't be faked as easily as marriages can.

"Tiffany," Magda says after a bite of cereal. "Can we play Monopoly?"

"Yes, honey," I reply absently as I return to the counter and grab myself a croissant from Ena's customary breakfast basket.

"And can we go see my pony?"

"Yes, honey."

"And can we go in the boat?"

I frown at the prospect. "Only if Mr. Ena agrees to take us."

"I can take you," Vadim pitches in, his tone cautious. I glance over my shoulder and discover that his wariness is for a good reason. Magda's pleasant expression promptly sours.

"I don't want to go on the boat anymore," she declares, her tone an icy imitation of his cruelest drawl. Embodying his standoffish talent, she pushes back from the table and grabs It by his head, letting him dangle from her hand as she marches from the kitchen, presumably upstairs.

"Give her time," I warn him. Sure enough, when I turn around, he's frowning, his gaze distant.

"How could I be so foolish?"

"You were still worried about her," I point out. "She'll get over it. And…" I weigh my next words carefully and decide that they're relevant. "If you let her play with Ainsley again, she'll forgive you a lot faster."

He raises an eyebrow. "Are you suggesting bribery?"

I shrug and hold up my hands defensively. "What you call bribery, I call 'attending to her needs.' She's lonely. What will a little playdate hurt?"

"Try telling that to Maxim," he counters gruffly. "I'm sure he's convinced himself that I am Magdalene, playing dress-up in a child suit by now."

I have to snort at that, seriousness aside. "Save your feud with your brother for another day. As for now, give Magda time. You can start with not letting her scare you off. Take us on the water today."

"Will I be rewarded for being a good captain?" he wonders, his voice husky.

My cheeks catch fire, and it takes everything I have not to retort with something equally suggestive. "No sex talk around innocent ears," I warn, waggling my finger. "And we really need to come up with some kind of schedule or safe word if Magda is in the house. I'd rather not be startled awake in post-coital bliss by a seven-year-old again."

"Point taken. You go grab her, and I'll get the boat ready."

VADIM HAS an expert poker face when he wants to. His invisible wall can seem insurmountable, and I never want to taste a fraction of the wrath he directs Maxim's way.

Magda inherited all of his skills of icy brooding and then some.

She scowls during the entire boat ride, letting her guise slack only in the rare moments when she thinks no one is watching. Only then does awe peek through her icy exterior, triggered by some aspect of the scenery or another. The property itself really is beautiful—a paradise nestled in the shadow of the sprawling metropolis that is Fair Haven. There are so many ways for Vadim to enhance the place, creating an oasis for Magda to thrive in.

That is, if she'll let him.

She maintains her stony silence when we return to the house for dinner. When I grab the Monopoly box, she crosses her arms and storms upstairs once it's clear that Vadim plans to participate.

"I'll go get her," I volunteer with a sigh. But Vadim rises to his feet, passing me.

"No. I will."

I swallow hard and follow him up to her room. She's stewing on the bed, and her glare darkens when she sees him.

"We should talk," he says, sitting on the edge of her bed. "I'm sorry I disappointed you. I promised you I would take you riding. I should have upheld that promise. You have every right to be upset with me."

"Why?" Magda demands. I flinch at the venom in her tone.

"Because I want you to trust me," Vadim says firmly.

"Trust you?" she scoffs, her tiny body radiating with increasing fury. "I hate you!"

"Magda!" I step forward, but Vadim raises his hand, and I stop short.

"Why?" he asks. "You have every right to hate me, but I would like to know why." His tone is so unnervingly gentle. She can't resist it.

"*Why?* Because you're a liar!" She lurches to her feet. Even while standing on the bed, she barely manages to tower above him. "I'm not stupid!" she shrieks, her voice losing any aspect of maturity. In this moment, she is all of seven. A hurt, brooding, wounded seven.

"I'm not stupid! I'm not!" She brandishes It by his floppy head, his body jerking wildly.

"Of course, you're not," Vadim murmurs. "I know that—"

"No, you don't!" She grasps It's body in one hand and brutally rips off his head with the other. The violence is tempered only by the tears spilling down her cheeks. She throws the bear's head aside and plunges her hand into its limp body—but rather than stuffing, she withdraws a folded slip of paper. "I know who you are," she says, sobbing openly. "I know! I saw papers in Mr. Robinson's office. Money that he got from some stupid company.

I googled it, and I saw your picture." She throws the slip of paper at Vadim.

His fingers shake as he unfurls it, revealing a faded printed photo of him in business attire.

"I waited for you," Magda snarls, her body heaving, her voice hitching. "I waited and waited and waited! You never came! You left me there! You left me with those people!" She puffs up, her face red, her expression so broken an answering tear falls down my cheek before I can wipe it away. "You didn't want me," she wails, pointing at him. "You didn't want me—"

"I wanted you." Vadim's tone is so fierce she falls silent in the face of it, her tiny shoulders slumping. I don't know who initiates the contact, but the next second, she's in his arms, her face in his chest, his fingers in her hair, loosening her braid. "More than anything," he grates against her scalp. "I wanted you..."

I back away the second Magda's tiny hands clutch him in return, sensing the need to make my exit. Downstairs I try to distract myself by cleaning up the table and the dirty dishes. Eventually, I wind up nursing a glass of wine, contemplating running.

This is best for everyone, right? A father and daughter reunited— no more need for an interloper...

After over an hour, I risk creeping up the stairs. A soothing, deep hum drifts from Magda's room. Singing? Yes. God, I recognize the rasping, haunting voice as Vadim's. He has her sleeping in his arms, rocking her as he sings the same song he must have while she was in the hospital.

My heart aches as I leave them be and crawl into bed alone.

If I were a better woman, I would gather my things and leave now. Let them rebuild their bond in peace. It might hurt in the short-term, but in the long-term, they'd be better off. They belonged together—without me.

But as the minutes tick by, I don't get up.

I never pack my things.

I never leave.

CHAPTER EIGHTEEN

I wake up, alarmed to realize that Vadim isn't beside me. Judging from the state of the sheets, he never came to bed during the entire night, either. When I venture down the hall, my alarm eases. I find him still in Magda's room, in the same position I'd left them in last night.

His eyes meet mine tiredly as she slumbers in his arms, her head propped against his shoulder.

Again, I retreat and shower, taking my time. I get dressed, and when I finally reemerge, Magda's room is empty. I head downstairs, but they aren't in the kitchen either. Or on the terrace.

Confused, I wander the rest of the downstairs level, only to run into a scowling Ena when I reach the front door.

"Horse," he grunts, though I sense he regrets telling me even that much.

I head out to the stables. Sure enough, the beautiful Zzazza is in one of the fenced-in pastures, looking like something out of a fairytale. Riding her is Vadim, still in his rumpled sweats. Seated before him, in her riding outfit, helmet in place, is Magda. She sits stiffly as he murmurs instructions into her ear, explaining various aspects of riding.

But bit by bit, she obeys his gentle suggestions, adjusting her grip on the reigns. And every now again, her eyes dart to him for approval—which she finds every single time.

My chest aches as I creep to the fence and watch them. It's a night and day contrast to yesterday. They both look relaxed, for one, their expressions neutral. Still hesitant in some ways, but it's progress.

Spotting me, Magda cracks the tiniest hint of something that may or may not be a smile, and my heart soars. Above her, Vadim grins in that wary, breathtaking way.

And their fragile, fledgling joy resonates like sunlight, adding life to the overcast landscape.

ONLY ONCE NIGHT FALLS, and Magda is fast asleep do I finally meet with Vadim alone. He enters the bedroom awkwardly, having been the one on bedtime duty for once.

Our eyes meet, and words spill from my throat before I can hold them back. "I'm so happy for you," I tell him, my voice wrought with emotion. "I am. I'm so, so happy—"

"But you're doubting." His eyes narrow as he advances, pinning me in against the wall before I even realize what's happening. One shift of his body and I'm trapped. But this prison isn't one

I'm eager to escape, no matter how fiercely every nerve in my body is urging me to run.

"My beauty…" My eyelids flutter as he grasps my chin, cradling my jaw against his palm. It should be illegal for one gesture to contain so much emotion. I sway, overwhelmed as he draws me to him, his mouth hovering near my throat.

"Gaining Magdalene was one obstacle I've surmounted," he tells me, his voice low with a determination that sets me alight. "I won't lose you. Whether I have to shackle you, or chastise or claim…" He captures my hips, grinding his touch into my flesh. "I refuse to relent. You *will* give in to me. I know it."

"Through marriage?" I ask softly.

He smiles, and my heart lurches, hammering madly. "Through corruption," he corrects, stroking my hair from my face. "I will corrupt you as thoroughly as you have tainted me, be it through marriage or otherwise."

"That sounds like a threat," I confess, even as I find myself lurching into him, manipulated by his groping touch.

"Take it as you will," he warns, his voice deepening with possession. "I will have you. No matter the cost. No matter the price. I will."

Whether I'm willing to be bought or not.

CHAPTER NINETEEN

"That's another round lost for Tiffany," Vadim declares from over a stack of neatly arranged Monopoly money. "I think we might have to up the stakes."

"Like what?" Magda asks conspiratorially. They sit on the same end of the table, far too close for my liking. Something tells me that I'm woefully outmatched in this war.

"Like…" Vadim cuts his gaze to me. "If Tiffany loses again, we should devise a fitting punishment for her."

"No fair!" I snatch a handful of money from the till and throw it at him. "I forfeit!"

Vadim's grin is sinful. "Shall we let her?" he asks Magda, who gleefully shakes her head, her curls bouncing.

"Then, I declare…" He strokes his chin in chilling contemplation. "That she be tickled to death!"

He lunges for me, and I race away, cackling at the top of my lungs. "No! I'll never give in! Never—"

I break off as a knock sounds from the front door, and I skid to a stop at the mouth of the foyer.

Frowning, Vadim slips past me, the playful mood broken. Squaring his shoulders, he opens the door, and I can tell just from his posture alone who he expects to be on the other end. His brother. "Shit, Ena didn't tell me that anyone…"

He trails off at the sight of the figure on the other end. As he steps back, alarm shoots through me at his expression. I've never seen his eyes so wide. So…open. It's as if he's seen a ghost.

And maybe he has.

The beautiful woman in the doorway is pale enough to have come from some ethereal realm. Curling blond hair falls down her shoulders, stopping almost at her waist. Delicate features form a face of breathtaking perfection, crowned by two intense light-blue eyes that fixate solely on the man between us.

"Irina," Vadim croaks.

"Vadim," she says, her voice softly accented. "I came to see our daughter."

<u>Vadim's story continues in Conquer! Read now!</u>

A WORD FROM THE AUTHOR

Hey there!

Thank you so much for reading! If you enjoyed the story, please leave a review and recommend the book to any friend you think would love this twisted world. You'd have my eternal gratitude. Even a short sentence goes a long way!

Then, come join the rest of us dark romance lovers in my Facebook Group where you can get snippets, sneak peeks of upcoming books and even help vote on aspects of future novels.

Come to the dark side:
https://www.facebook.com/groups/lanasbeautifulmonsters/

WANT MORE STUFF TO READ?
Join my newsletter and get a **free book**! Plus, you get to stay updated with any new releases, random giveaways and exclusive sneak peeks!
https://www.lanaskybooks.com/newsletter

Other Novels: https://lanaskybooks.com/

FREE BOOK - JOIN MY NEWSLETTER

Dark, Twisted Romance

Join my newsletter and get a **free book**! Plus, you get to stay updated with any new releases, random giveaways and exclusive sneak peeks!

https://www.lanaskybooks.com/newsletter

ABOUT THE AUTHOR

Lana Sky is a reclusive writer in the United States who spends most of her time daydreaming about complex male characters and parenting her Cockapoo Joey. She writes dark, twisted romance across several genres. Her titles include everything from mafia romance to vampires.

facebook.com/AuthorLanaSky

twitter.com/lanasky101

amazon.com/author/lanasky

pinterest.com/lanasky101

goodreads.com/lanasky

instagram.com/lanasky101

bookbub.com/authors/lana-sky

ALSO BY LANA SKY

For more titles by Lana Sky, please visit:

https://www.lanaskybooks.com